The
Library Diaries

Ann Miketa

PublishAmerica
Baltimore

ISBN: 1-60563-568-5
PUBLISHED BY PUBLISHAMERICA, LLLP
www.publishamerica.com
Baltimore

Printed in the United States of America

This book is dedicated with gratitude and love to Judy—Grand Matriarch of the Judirosa, Pittsboro, North Carolina, whose unconditional love, support, and sense of humor pulled me through the Gates of Hell and showed me I had a life to live, and to my son, Myles, the light of my life.

Table of Contents

Prologue 11

Introduction 17

Chapter One: Destination Hell 21

Chapter Two: Mr. Three Hats, a.k.a. the Hovercraft 25

Chapter Three: Diane 29

Chapter Four: Mr. Waterman 36

Chapter Five: The After-Hours Pervert 38

Chapter Six: The Clown Pervert 40

Chapter Seven: The Handicapped Pervert 43

Chapter Eight: The Masturbator 47

Chapter Nine: The Bonkers 49

Chapter Ten: Craziest of the Crazy Mothers 52

Chapter Eleven: Horny Old Men 55

Chapter Twelve: Wall of Bums 63

Chapter Thirteen: The Yucks 66

Chapter Fourteen: Leeanne 68

Chapter Fifteen: Beth 72

Chapter Sixteen: Garden-Variety Drunks and Crazies 76

Chapter Seventeen: Strychnine 80

Chapter Eighteen: Genealogy 84

Chapter Nineteen: Millennium 87

Chapter Twenty: Lying Patrons 90

Chapter Twenty-One: Leon 93

Chapter Twenty-Two: The Do-It-Yourself-Divorce (If I Only
Had the Brains) Patrons 95

Chapter Twenty-Three: Mr. Magoo 98
Chapter Twenty-Four: Greedy, Unenlightened Patrons 104
Chapter Twenty-Five: Book Writers 106
Chapter Twenty-Six: Christian Fiction 110
Chapter Twenty-Seven: Board Ethics 115
Chapter Twenty-Eight: Paper Thief 120
Chapter Twenty-Nine: Hunters as Conservationists............. 122
Chapter Thirty: Short People, Stiff People 125
Chapter Thirty-One: Strange Requests, Odd Situations 127
Chapter Thirty-Two: Becca's Transformation 133
Epilogue 136
About the Author 143

"We must be willing to get rid of the life we've planned, so as to have the life that is waiting for us."

~Joseph Campbell

The
Library Diaries

Prologue

Did Joseph Campbell have any idea how difficult this little bit of wisdom could be? My sister, Moriah, who wrote the diary that I turned into the book, *The Library Diaries,* knew from personal experience just how hard it was to give up ones hopes, dreams, and plans and make the best of another, very different life. Really, our entire family, because of several bad decisions and indiscretions made by our parents, had to re-adjust our expectations of life. Like they say in the 12-Step programs, one needs to "keep one's expectations low, and one's acceptance high."

Moriah and I were only a year apart, so we shared every single detail regarding our hopes and plans for the future. It never entered our minds, as it shouldn't have to enter any child's mind, that, the security our parents provided for us would one day be pulled out from under us before we were ready to "leave the nest."

I was a sophomore in high school; "Rye" (Moriah's nickname) a junior. There followed four younger brothers, all of us only a year apart. Rye and I had plans to go to college. We grew up on the East Coast in a wonderful, liberal college town. We had high ideals about life, and both of us sought to make the world a better place. We were children of the sixties, albeit, the cusp of.

When the "shit hit the fan," our family lost everything. As I said, my parents made several ill-considered decisions that led to us losing our house, the main source of security for a family. Our mother's drinking accelerated, our parents divorced, our mother retreated to her room, and would not come out, even though she had school-age children, and my dad moved to a condo and started dating young women my age.

My sister and I moved in with a friend whose mother was on academic sabbatical from the university. From there, we easily fell into using drugs and alcohol just to feel normal. We were trying to get back to the way we felt before our lives fell apart, before everything we had believed became a fallacy. While we spiraled into emotional disarray, we were aware of our friends preparing for college. We were trying to come to terms with the fact that we were stuck. We had stopped attending all of the extra-curricular activities we had been involved in and started working after school and on weekends, hoping to earn enough money to attend college.

We had been raised in a liberal, East Coast college town. All of our friends' parents were professors, lawyers, or medical professionals. We knew there were many problems in the world, even though our community was not directly affected by them. Our friends' parents, along with our own, had taught us to be aware of and involved in the world. It was assumed we would all go out, change the world, and make it better.

But you know when bad things happen, it's not so easy to maintain these high, noble ideas. Bone-crushing poverty and mind-numbing work challenge us to stay positively focused.

Rye and I both managed to attend college, not the fancy, private schools we had hoped and planned for, but our local liberal arts college. Sadly, before Rye graduated from high school, she fell in love with the wrong guy. After the rug was pulled out from under us, we all reacted in different ways. I think Rye needed the security that being in love can give to a person who is feeling as disconnected as we all were. She became pregnant, had a wonderful, healthy little boy, but ended up having to raise him herself. It was painful watching her struggle with their day-to-day existence. She ended up having to go on welfare, which was the most humiliating experience any of us could ever think of having to go through. She would drive her old Saab thirty miles away so no one she knew would see her use her food stamps. I helped her as much as I could, but I could see the hopelessness and bitterness descending upon her. She was a lovely, kind, smart young woman who had made a bad decision that would change not only her whole life but who she was.

She raised her little boy from birth until he was four years old by herself. Then she met and fell in love with a stable, emotionally available man who was not afraid of commitment. The only problem was he was planning to move, and not only to move, but to move to the Midwest, the antithesis of her hometown and everything and everyone she loved.

She came to accept that she wasn't going to be one of the lucky ones who were able to have their lives just the way they want. Most of us simply take for granted that we'll get to live where we want to live, have the great spouse and the fulfilling job, but it is not so for all of us. She held her head high, fought back the tears, and gave us all reassuring smiles and hugs as she said goodbye. We all glared at what we viewed as "the Neanderthal man dragging her away by her hair."

Of course she and I kept in close contact. Rye's talents and education lay in dance, theater, and music, so it seemed a double crime that she would end up in a small, rural Midwestern town. She landed a job at the local public library, and from the start she would call to tell me the library stories. She felt as though she had moved to a different planet. As the years went by, she had encountered so many not only bizarre people and situations working there, but a new outlook on life. Her experiences working there had totally transformed her. I told her she needed to write these stories and events down. Eventually, I mentioned to her she needed to write a book. None of us could believe the stuff she was telling us had occurred at the library was really happening. I didn't know at the time that she had, in fact, starting writing a book.

After living in her new home fifteen years, my sister was diagnosed with lung cancer. She was diagnosed in January and had died by the middle of March. While being with her throughout her last months of life, she told me about her book. She told me she never got around to hunting for an agent or publisher, but that if I wanted to pursue getting her book published after she died she would like that.

I read the book completely a week after my sister's death. I loved it. I asked a few friends to read it and they felt the same way.

So this is how *The Library Diaries* came to be. I only wish my sister were here to continue the stories.

Introduction

The primary reason for my writing this book is to share the stories of the characters you are about to meet. After working at a public library in a small, rural Midwestern town (which I will refer to as Denialville, Michigan, throughout this book) for fifteen years, I have encountered strains and variations of crazy I didn't know existed in such significant portions of our population.

The second reason is because of how the library experience has profoundly changed me. I do not seem to be anything like the person I was when I moved to Denialville fifteen years ago, leaving a wonderful East Coast college town in North Carolina. This dramatic change has caused me to speculate on how much how we were brought up, where we grew up, and what we were taught can hinder us from realizing some of the outstanding characteristics of the American population. Until a person leaves the ivory-tower existence inherent to the liberal college town, one really doesn't know the composition of the majority of our society.

And finally, it's been said to write about what we know, the familiar.

I was raised in a large, Catholic, upper-middle-class family. My parents were crazy over the Kennedys and sincerely believed we should give to anyone in need. I have maintained these beliefs into adulthood, never thinking, like my parents before me, that it is important for people to help themselves. We never stopped to think that our social programs might be producing a significant population who could not survive without being completely dependent on its government or that we were not only permitting but encouraging people who should never have kids to bear children. Many women who have multiple babies they can't take care of view motherhood as their only option and define themselves simply as these babies' mothers. They may have never had the love, support, and care we all need from our primary caregivers (parents) so they have babies, hoping, as a result, they will have someone to love and who will love them back, but shortly after giving birth, find the responsibility overwhelming.

In the town in which I grew up, I don't think anyone was on welfare. There may have been a few recipients, but only for a short time during a rough period, not as a way of life. Here in Denialville, Michigan, third- and fourth-generation welfare families are common. They don't see a thing wrong with being on welfare or exhibiting a variety of other dysfunctional behaviors. Another way many locals look at outrageous and dysfunctional behavior is to excuse it with, "Well, that's who they are, so we need to love them as they are." It's like someone having cancer and being told, "Well, that's what you have, so just accept it."

My fear is that we are giving endlessly to a growing population of mentally impaired people and not giving enough to the middle-class population. In two-parent families where both parents work, unless they're highly paid professionals, sending their kids to college has to be done with student and parent loans at eight-percent interest. Our government just raised interest on Parent Plus loans for college to eight percent in an effort to balance the federal budget. Once again the middle class is expected to carry the financial burden while our wages do not increase. My husband's a high-school teacher, and as you know, I work at a public library. He has not had a salary increase in three years, and I will normally get a one-percent raise. We have had to borrow all of the funds for our kids' college educations, but the growing numbers of impaired people continue to receive more and more benefits.

A lot of the individuals you will meet in my book simply have low IQs. There might be something in the water here, or else something just isn't quite right in their thinking, so they get disability of some sort, but they often have children who are mentally or emotionally impaired. This isn't just one or two individuals. At any time in the library, at least half of the individuals here are not able to join the work force and support themselves because of some type of mental condition. I have to wonder why no one ever stops to ask why. Why are there so many mentally handicapped people, and why, why, why are they allowed to have children who they can't take care of? Some may say this sounds mean spirited. What is mean spirited? Simply not having children since you are not mentally accomplished, cannot support yourself, and cannot provide a child with what it needs or going ahead and having a child even though you can't take care of it? Hollywood's portrayal of Forrest Gump is very heart-warming and cute but not realistic. Plus, Forrest did not have criminal tendencies like so many low-IQ individuals do, especially the ones with fetal alcohol syndrome (FAS). I see kids born with FAS every day at the library. No other kids want to be around them because they do not possess the social skills nor IQ's to be desired friends and sadly, almost always they come from poor, uneducated parents who also have FAS.

We need to be willing to say something to parents, especially mothers, who drink or drug while they are carrying their children. We will end up paying for the child, and the child will not stand a chance at a normal, decent life, no matter how much money we pour into their sad families. I can meet a child in kindergarten at the library and know he or she will end up being a criminal.

Let's brainstorm and come up with better ways to help people besides throwing money to them. It hasn't worked well for the past fifty years.

It is time to meet the library patrons.

Chapter One
Destination Hell

Destination Hell is my nickname for a crazy but delightful old woman who comes to our library. She is around seventy-five, somewhat crouched over, always wears some type of kerchief over her head tucked beneath a camel colored coat. She usually has on polyester pants with some type of pattern, and has an orange-colored cloth purse slung over her body like women wear these days. Geneva recently died, but her memory will live on forever.

Geneva was short and petite, but when she entered the library, a whirlwind of leaves, wind, and pine needles always came with her. It is almost always windy here in the Midwest on Lake Michigan. This is wind like you cannot imagine if you have never been in it, the type of wind that is the precursor to an East Coast storm, but this wind keeps going and doesn't stop. I call it gratuitous wind.

Geneva had been kicked off our mass transit system for bullying others and being verbally abusive. Geneva sometimes told it like it was a little too bluntly and had a tendency to reach out and clobber someone if he or she were irritating her.

You've got to be wondering how she acquired her nickname, Destination Hell. I hope you like this story, but I know I will not be able to do her justice in the telling.

As I have told you, I have worked in the library for fifteen years. The first five or so years we did not have computers, and the library was visited by significantly fewer perverts. We only had people who wanted to check out books rather than look at pornography or search for mail-order brides or aliens from other planets. Believe me, having computers in public libraries is terribly overrated. Most parents with kids should be able to afford a computer at home (or maybe they should have had fewer kids) so most kids do their homework on computers at home. Don't most of the people you know have their own computers?

Well, we got our computers. One day a couple of high school kids were sitting among a pod of computers. Geneva came whirling into the library. She almost always had a lot of bags with books in them. She proceeded to sit down next to one of the high-school kids, who happened to have the word "DESTINATION" written in the address bar (these were older computers). Geneva looked up and blurted out very loudly, "HELL. Type in HELL. That's the only destination I have ever known or been to." The cluster of high school kids just froze. It was as if E.F. Hutton had spoken. They looked bewildered, but Geneva just kept insisting he type it in and continued with her rant regarding her experiences of hell on earth.

Geneva had been married to a cop. She had been raised right outside of Denialville. She had been from a rural lower-middle-class family. She went to live with her aunt in Chicago. Oh, if you could hear how she said "Chicago" and how her eyes lit up when she talked about her life there when she was young. Basically her parents let her go live with her aunt because there weren't any opportunities for her here. She went to high school there and met her husband-to-be while he was on leave from the military. They met down by the Chicago docks at a bar. They married while he was in the service, and he became a cop. Geneva always said "cop," never "policeman." He died of a heart attack shortly after he retired, so by the time I met Geneva, she had been widowed for over twenty-five years. She had left Chicago and moved back here to Denialville and purchased a house. She told me about how "the pink piggies" (the cops and the men from the insane asylum) were always trying to take her away. My guess was that she probably had been unwillingly placed in a "crazy farm" for a while and was supposed to take some type of medicine. She wasn't a threat to herself or others. She lived fine on her own. She was certain someone was trying to steal her husband's two cars that had been parked in her yard since he died and she had moved. She said the kids in the neighborhood liked to place big firecrackers on the cars to blow them up. She told me the "pink piggies" broke both of her legs once to get her into their vehicle to take her to the "crazy farm." Once I asked her if she was getting enough food. I was going to mention she could receive meals from Meals on Wheels. Her response: "SLOP! It's all they have. SLOP! If I wanted SLOP, I could make that at home."

Another fantastically dramatic Geneva moment; she came whirling once again into the library. You have to understand the energy components when she came in. Most of the staff ran to the back to avoid her. But I liked her. She was interesting. I could see the determination in her walk and sense her mind was working on something. She arrived at the front desk, out of breath, since she had to walk everywhere she needed to go, leaned on the desk, and yelled, "This town is like a Babylonian whore! They're all Babylonian whores! They'll sell you and yours to the highest bidder!" See, her mind was always working.

Her son, who lived in Chicago, had not been to visit her in over ten years.

The last time she was in the library she told me this would probably be the last time I saw her since she felt like she was going to die soon. I asked her if I could take her to see a doctor. Her response: "Quacks, they're all quacks!" She wanted to die as she had lived, on her own terms.

Chapter Two
Mr. Three Hats, a.k.a. the Hovercraft

Mr. Three Hats is not Native American as you may have assumed by his name. No, Mr. Three Hats simply wore three hats no matter what the weather or where he was going. On most days, he wore a stocking cap, a parka top, and another stocking cap on the top. Now when I say parka top-I mean the detachable part of a parka—so the sides of the hat were always flapping out on both sides. No matter what the weather—be it 30 below (which it gets here) or 90—he wore the hats. When it was warm outside, he would have on a short-sleeve shirt and the three hats.

He also had bags of stuff with him all the time. All kinds of food stuff, extra shoes—we never knew what else.

Rodney (Three Hats' name) came from a family of four siblings. I don't know anything about the parents, but the four siblings lived in a very nice part of town, on a lake area with acreage, a much nicer house in a much nicer area than a teacher and library worker could ever afford. All four siblings were on disability. Rodney and his sister Rhea were regular library patrons. Rodney came on a daily, sometimes all-day basis, Rhea about once a month. They were both bright, though Rodney had some type of screw loose; both could work some type of job. One of the other siblings, whom I have never met but whose goal in life was to capture Bigfoot, was an official Bigfoot hunter. He had a truck with a camper on it that said, BIGFOOT HUNTER. I heard from Rodney's neighbors that he mostly pursued Bigfoot in Montana. But dear reader, we were paying for those endeavors with our tax dollars.

Now Rodney liked to play the stock market on our computers. He would holler, "God damn it!" whenever something came up he didn't like. We had other patrons who complained regularly about Rodney's behavior, but my director never let us kick Rodney out. He and some of the other nutbuckets simply got to stay, act crazy, and run the other people out. Of course, the other people were generally taxpayers who were paying for the library, including the computers. Rodney also complained to us about how slow our computers were—as did most of the perverts who used them. I said, "You know what? They're free!" I have even mentioned to a few individuals that if they wanted a faster computer connection they might consider getting a job or taking a night job and putting one on store credit, just like I had to do. Gateway will accommodate anyone, no matter what the income.

Can you imagine complaining to a library that is offering you a FREE service about that very service, especially when you don't contribute anything financially to support it? At one point, Rodney had such a negative relationship with one of our patrons, whose story I will tell you later, that our director set up scheduled times when Rodney could be there and other times for the other patron. Rodney's sister called at the library asking us to tell Rodney when it was time to come home.

I cannot tell you how shocked I was upon learning that Rodney drove. He drove and could play the stock market, so why not work? My family would never be able to afford stock, yet I am supporting someone who can? Go figure.

Rodney's sister Rhea told me once what was wrong with Rodney, something about his blood not having the necessary elements in it, so he was always cold.

Before the showdown with the other patron, Rodney was in the library all day, every day. Initially, computer use was simply a free for all. That's how our director wanted it. I knew that was a huge mistake. So Rodney would simply get on a computer; then when someone else signed up to use the one he was on, he would "hover around" all the other computers waiting for someone else to finish, and then he would hop on, hence, the name, Hovercraft. Our director allowed him to do this for several years until, finally, enough patrons complained about having this weirdo hovering around them and looking over their shoulders, along with passively intimidating them to hurry up so he could get on the computer. I suggested to my director that we just give Rodney one of our old computers so he could take it home, use it there, and not come to the library. My co-workers and I spend an extraordinary amount of time and emotional energy negotiating computer use with patrons, Rodney in particular. And as I mentioned before, they are using library computers for pornography, mail-order brides, singles clubs, and sometimes trying to contact Al Qaeda or citizens from other planets. The kids who come in usually will play games on the computers for hours if permitted.

Chapter Three
Diane

Diane is an American woman who had been married to a Norwegian. She and her son had lived in Norway for twenty years or so when they showed up at our library. I was never quite clear what brought them here. Her story was layered between some murder that had been committed and the two of them running away from her Norwegian ex-husband. The stories were so fascinating that I really didn't find it annoying at all to have her sitting next to my desk at the library talking to me for hours.

I never knew what was true and what wasn't. She told me her ex-husband had murdered someone here in America because the person knew too much about a crime committed in Norway. Her ex-spouse apparently had been quite wealthy and his family rather prominent. Her son's grandparents, according to her, had been molesting her son for years. Her parents lived here in the US and knew about the molestations, but the father's wealthy parents had paid them since the beginning of the molestations to keep quiet. Apparently there was an ongoing child molestation ring her son and his dad were involved in.

I don't know if any of this is true. No one else seemed to believe her, but I felt there was some truth there somewhere. When I asked the son, he did not give specifics, but he did confirm that most of what his mom said was true.

I guessed Diane had some personality disorder, because of behavior I will later speak of, and needed to talk with a good therapist. Diane was an extremely bright and beautiful forty-ish-year-old with a very vibrant personality and wit.

I asked her many times how she ended up in tiny, rural Denialville. She told me an agency had provided a safe place for her and her son to live in here in Denialville. She and her son were placed in a home with an apparently turbo-Christian family. I guess someone was hoping that with the help of the Lord, all Diane and her son's problems would vanish. Isn't it strange the way so many people think that the Lord really will make mental illness go away? We have the ability to study the brain and mind well enough to devise medicines and therapies to deal with mental illnesses to the point that most people with mental illness can lead close to normal lives if they take their medications.

Well, it turns out Diane did not get along with these sponsors. Diane had been trying to get disability for some time, maybe several years. She had a cluster of physical illnesses, including lupus and severe arthritis, that would have made working full time difficult. Her son worked various jobs, though jobs are scarce here and wages are terrible—think minimum wage. So they had to continue to live together, since Diane could not support herself. Her son was probably twenty-three, not an age when a young man wants to live with his mom, but he could not just abandon her. One of the requirements for anyone receiving disability is going through a physical and mental evaluation by a physician chosen by the Social Security Administration. This Diane absolutely refused to do. It wasn't the physical evaluation she objected to but the psychiatric evaluation. This refusal brought warning signs to my mind. I mentioned to Diane that she really didn't have anything to lose, and that they required this of everyone applying for disability, and so what if they diagnosed a mental imbalance? If it got her disability what would it matter? She really did not have anything to lose. Her son was grown, so they couldn't take him from her. She was unemployed and was not looking for employment. They didn't own anything and moved every three months or so because Diane would become dissatisfied with something or other about their current rental. Diane stayed at the library all day, every day. She sometimes slept on one of the couches in one of our private meeting rooms. She was so afraid of being diagnosed with some sort of mental imbalance that she was willing to simply forgo her chances of qualifying for disability.

I am amazed and dumbfounded by how terrified people here

in Denialville are to talk about, much less acknowledge, mental illness.

I have had depression for over half my life. I come from a community where just about three quarters of the population have depression at some point in their lives. How could one look at the world realistically and not be depressed?

The absolutely horrifying job most parents do at raising their kids has produced a plethora of borderline personality problems. I would say at least every other person who enters our library has some type of personality disorder, and they and their families walk around in total oblivion and denial with a path of destruction behind them, usually the destruction of an innocent, dependent child. But instead of looking around objectively and realizing that their lives are not moving along the same or a similar course like the rest of the world and making some changes, they just keep going somehow. When a person can't hold down a job for more than a few weeks, or when a family's kids are constantly in trouble at school, it's not the employer's or the school's fault. It's the parents' fault.

So Diane refused the evaluation. She totally disagreed with a person taking medicine for any type of illness that might have its roots in a reaction to the behavior of others. For instance, with depression or other mood disorders, background could possibly play a small or very large part in the disorder. Diane said it was wrong for the victim to be the one to have to go to therapy and take the medicine. I felt like I had run into a brick wall with Diane after hearing her say this. There was no getting through to someone with this attitude. And how does one get this attitude? I know when I finally got it together enough to see that I was painfully unhappy, when I couldn't keep from crying every day, that I had to do something for myself, I found people who could and would help me. I loved these people. They not only cared about me but also had the medical background to get me started with anti-depressants. It was like a huge grey cloud that had followed me most of my life simply vanished. I could see opportunities and options. My therapist gave me an IQ test, because several members of my family had either told me I was dumb or alluded to the fact. Even though I had been in and out of college I still felt inferior to others academically and intellectually. These therapists knew I was bright and knew I would only believe it if I were tested.

Why was Diane so willing to admit to many physical ailments but not the possibility of a mental ailment? Why is this town of Denialville, with more bars and tattoo parlors than any town I have ever lived in, along with a tremendous amount of alcoholism and illiteracy, unwilling to admit that something's the matter?

Diane's view of the victim reminds me of a similar attitude my dad has. He suffers from bi-polar disorder, alcoholism, and co-dependency, having grown up in an alcoholic home himself. He is a white-collar professional in medicine and refuses to take any medicine for any of his disorders since, after all, anyone that's been though what he's been through would be depressed.

Diane and Mr. Three Hats eventually became adversaries. One of the problems was that they were both here at the library every day, all day. It seems some people start believing they can take inappropriate liberties with another person if they are in the same public place all day every day. They start feeling like, or thinking that they have a relationship with someone simply because they are in the same building all day together. As I have said, Diane is very attractive. She had problems with men ogling her. I am out in the front lines of our library. I am the only one out on the floor all day seeing what is happening. I saw many of the old horny geezers who hang out at the library just staring at her or simply thinking they could walk up to her and talk with her, since she was there all the time. I personally don't want anyone acting that familiar with me unless I know them well. None of these old geezers knew Diane except for seeing her in the library.

Then Mr. Three Hats started following her around in the library. Diane finally exploded. I am surprised she didn't explode sooner. She demanded that something be done about the stalking and ogling. No one should have been permitted to stalk her. I had let my director know several times when men had made advances toward her, and nothing was done. Then, when she finally did explode, Mr. Three Hats and Diane were told they couldn't be in the library at the same time. They had to split the day. Diane didn't agree with the new rule, so, she ignored it and visited the library when she wanted. The police were called. She was handcuffed and taken into custody. I don't know what happened to her. I don't know if charges were pressed, but she has never been in the library again (her choice) and will not speak to me when I see her.

The handling of Diane was odd to me. We have child molesters and all sorts of individuals with criminal sexual assault records who use our library, even when there are children present. I have seen various men rubbing themselves inappropriately while looking at women in the library and have reported it to my director, and his view is that if the patron doesn't come in and make a complaint, he can't do anything, never even getting up to see who the person was. But here we have a bright, attractive, opinionated, outspoken woman letting the world know how screwed up it is, and she gets kicked out, handcuffed no less.

Personally, I prefer her craziness to the perverts who come into the library, trying to act like they are normal, by talking with women all nice and jokingly when, in reality, they've been let out of prison on child-molestation charges.

Check your sexual offender registry, and then check your local library. I'll bet at least half of the listed perps hang out there. Each state has its own registry.

Chapter Four
Mr. Waterman

Mr. Waterman's real name was Mr. Waterman, but the fact that he came into the library with empty gallon jugs to get water was more than just ironically funny. It was just too perfect.

Mr. Waterman was a Vietnam veteran. The other veterans in our area told me his story. They all looked out for each other, as it should be.

Mr. Waterman suffered from both shell shock and too much illegal drug use. He came in pretty much daily. He took our mass transit, Dial-A-Ride, into town, sat right next to my desk, and read the papers, only he didn't read them, he rhymed them out loud.

He took the headlines from numerous papers, jumbled them around, and turned them into a type of beat-poet rhyme, somewhat like Ferlinghetti, the same meter. And if you listened closely, you could make out these erratic word associations and commentary. And every time, never fail, he came up to the front desk and asked us to call Dial-A-Ride for him to 950 Jebavy. He always said thank you, too.

Chapter Five
The After-Hours Pervert

We have ongoing problems with perverts looking at porn on our computers. We have added the required by state blocks, but people still know how to get to their porn and sexual deviance locations.

Over the span of several days, maybe even a couple weeks, we saw a tremendous amount of porn usage. It was finally figured out that someone was in the library building after hours, on the Internet, watching porn for hours.

So when we closed at eight o'clock at night we had to go up to the attic and check every room, every nook and cranny to make sure the pervert wasn't there. None of us ever found him. We thought maybe he/she entered through a window after hours.

That was until one evening when one of our female employees needed to come to the library later at night for something. In her pajamas, she came through the employee door, walked out into the library, noticed a lit area in the children's section to her right, looked and saw a man on the computer in the kids' section. They saw each other, and he ran. She called either our director or the police—probably both.

The after-hours pervert was easily caught. He had numerous prior arrests. He is another of the crazies, no doubt raised by crazy parents, now a sex offender who keeps getting a slap on the wrist and let out.

I can't remember the exact number of long-distance calls he made to access porn over the internet, but it was several thousand dollars. Night after night, he would sit at one of our computers and look at porn. As we all know, this wasn't just plain old sex, this consisted of bestiality along with all kinds of other sexual deviances. Really, stop and think about the types of minds these people have and how dangerous they are to society. How would any one of us respond if one of these people sexually assaulted or raped one of our children? The chances are pretty good that this could happen. But all we do is sit and watch them lurk around us.

What does a person do with the sexual arousal produced after watching porn for hours?

The after-hours pervert sometimes sat at my desk, in my chair, using my computer. I told my boss that I just could not bring myself to sit in that chair anymore. Who knows what kinds of body fluids may have leaked out of him. Thankfully, he let me go buy a new chair that same day.

Chapter Six
The Clown Pervert

The clown pervert resembled a clown. He, like most of the other perverts, had a blank flatness to his eyes, and something was off kilter in his facial features. The clown pervert was in his late sixties to early seventies and may have been on disability his whole adult life.

To the undiscerning eye, he might have appeared normal. I have learned that most people don't notice their surroundings. I have always been acutely aware of everything and everyone around me. I have radar for the slightest mental or physical anomaly. I could tell just by looking at this guy that something wasn't right.

The clown pervert was soft-spoken, so one was taken off guard when he made his perverted requests. Bald on top with tufts of grey, wispy, wiry hair on the sides, like a clown, he also had big eyes and that somewhat goofy smile that hides craziness behind it.

He came slithering into the library one day with a perverted request for books with pictures of women having sex with each other. I was at my desk, which is about fifteen feet from the front desk, where patrons normally go for questions or to check books in or out. He had already gone to the front desk. Of course he did not have the sense or intelligence to find what he needs by himself, nor did he realize how inappropriate his request was.

I looked up to see the high-school page, who was working the front desk, her face and ears beet red with embarrassment. She wasn't really sure what this person was trying to find, and he was making her uncomfortable.

So I went over to the desk to help him, asked him what he needed to find, and he told me, "I'm looking for a book of girls and sex."

In an effort to understand what he meant, I asked, "Do you mean women's sexuality, sexual education, or awareness?"

"No," he replied, "I mean something with pictures in it of girls and sex."

It was beginning to dawn on me that another pervert was among us, but still not sure what he is seeking, I continued to probe the pervert's mind by asking, "Do you want something more about how to have or enjoy sex?"

Without batting an eye or showing any sign or embarrassment

he said, "I'm looking for a book with pictures of women having sex with each other."

Without reaching over and smacking the goofy smile off his face, and with my most diplomatic voice I told him, "Well, that's not something we would normally have available here at the library; you might check at the book store."

Then to top it all off he said, "You mean pay for a book?"

I just looked at him with restrained hatred and walked away.

How do parents raise someone who has so little awareness of what is socially acceptable? Yes, he was mentally ill, but do we really want to or have to put up with his perversions? Apparently, those of us who work in public places do. And there is nothing endearing about these people. They have lived sad, limited, unproductive, parasitic lives. Some will certainly do others harm.

Chapter Seven
The Handicapped Pervert

This particular pervert had the misfortune of being in a wheelchair. One day he came wheeling into the library, stopping at our copying machine. As I watched the interaction he was having with the high-school girl at the desk, I noticed she was looking rather stunned, so I headed over there. She told me she was being made uncomfortable with what this particular patron was requesting of her.

He wanted to have some copies made of nude women. Now remember folks, there are many other places where a person can get copies made. There are even do-it-yourself copiers, which would have been a much more appropriate place for the handicapped pervert to get his copies made.

He was totally unaware of how his behavior might affect and was affecting the young woman who was waiting on him. He could have avoided this by simply going to the post office or the local chain gas station and using their self-service machines.

I told him that we wouldn't be making copies for him at a library and suggested other places that had self service copiers. I told him he had embarrassed the underage high-school girl with his inappropriate request. Then he told me he was an artist and needed the pictures for his artwork. I assured him I was really not interested or concerned over what he was using them for.

Then, as usual, the squeaky wheel got the grease. He wheeled into my director's office, complained to my director, and my director agreed to make his copies. I have to take a moment and say that I think it is really important for managers/directors to back their employees whenever possible and appropriate. Not doing so only encourages the aggressive pests of the population who always get squeaky when they are told they can't do something. Thus, the squeaky wheel does get the grease.

This incident brought about a discussion over how my director and I disagreed in our idea over appropriate behavior. Are we, as a society, not allowed to count on, expect, and rely on others to maintain a degree of socially appropriate behavior? Do we not have any measuring stick to use? Is there not any sort of understanding toward what is expected of a person if he or she chooses to be part of society? I mentioned to my boss that perhaps no one had ever modeled appropriate behavior for this person, and it was up to us, meaning the world he lived in and the people he encountered, to teach him.

Well, you can guess what came next. That ridiculous R-word, *relativism*! He noted that none of us were really qualified or in a position to declare what is acceptable behavior and what wasn't, since we all came from different backgrounds, and that I, with my upper- middle-class background, had different expectations and perceptions of the world.

To me, we might as well say, "Well, considering he grew up in the slums and used children as shields to keep from being murdered, then it's okay if he does that with my kid, too, since that's what is considered normal to him. That's typical for the environment he grew up in."

What promotes positive change in most people is an awareness that their behavior, their lack of success emotionally, socially, intellectually, financially, or spiritually is causing them to feel out of sync with the world. The ones who do not or cannot arrive at that awareness, because of a lack of good parenting, drug addiction or other kinds of addictions, or just too low an IQ to evolve into a whole person, don't ever change. As long as we make concessions to accommodate their inappropriate behaviors, we take away any and all reason for them to change. A willingness to change almost has to be forced upon people. Poverty, misery, sadness, depression, these are all states of being that, when suffered long enough, should catapult us into changing, no matter what the cost.

Have you ever noticed that losers gravitate towards losers, addicts to addicts, beer-drinking hell raisers to beer-drinking hell raisers? That's where they are most comfortable. They have got to be made uncomfortable eventually so that change can come over them.

"Relativism" too often is a term for accepting unacceptable behavior.

Chapter Eight
The Masturbator

One day, as I was working the front reference desk with several of the high-school kids, a woman made a point of requesting that I help her. She let me know that she had a problem she didn't want to share with the younger employees.

This woman was in her late forties, mother to a grown child of about age twenty-three, who masturbated almost constantly. This, sadly, is not a joke.

He would masturbate to the point of ejaculation. She, for years, had been cleaning up his semen not only from his bed but from many other surfaces around their house.

I asked her if her son was in therapy for this. She was just, finally, considering taking him to therapy. He was twenty-three and rarely ever left the house.

This woman looked totally exhausted. I said to her that I

thought the move to therapy was really the best she could do, not only for him but for her, too.

Why she hadn't admitted something was wrong and gotten help before that moment was the question I wanted most to ask. She told me she and her mother, the boy's grandma, had not spoken since her son was a little boy because the grandma had told the mother early on, when the boy was little, that he needed therapy. The mother took offense to this, so they hadn't spoken for years.

I had mixed emotions toward this woman. I felt pity for her, but I wanted to scream at her at the same time. To have not found help for this child up until then just made me furious. She was looking for information on obsessive-compulsive disorder. So at least they had been to one therapy session where it was suggested she read up on obsessive-compulsive behavior.

I don't know if this is a small-town tendency to deny that something is the matter or accept unacceptable behavior as being part of who that person is. It is shocking to observe parents who are unwilling to get therapy for their children. In more progressive areas, parents would not hesitate to bring their child to a therapist. It is the same as bringing ones child to a physician. What causes this reluctance? I view it as poor, irresponsible, unenlightened, lazy parenting, and it is rampant.

Chapter Nine
The Bonkers

This family, if seated together would look like four Jabba the Hutts. Their bodies were totally glob-like. There were a mother, father, sister, and brother, and not one high-school diploma among the four. They checked out the GED book, but none of them had successfully taken the test. The library has had from fifty to one-hundred copies of the GED within the past ten years; all have been stolen. Personally, I cannot imagine why any one without a high school diploma would begin to think she or he had what it took to raise a child properly. Yes, occasionally you'll find an exception to the rule, and a person will have managed to lead a successful life without the high school diploma, but it is extremely rare. That person will not be able to help with homework or with the inevitable frustrations that life with kids bring a parent. They will not be able to support a child financially, much less be able to provide any of the extras. Raising a child in poverty is not fun. There is nothing quaint or cute about it. When ignorance is thrown in with the poverty, it creates a toxic environment for a child.

Maybe having sex shouldn't be so easy, since so many poor, ignorant people are having it without any birth control. I would love to have had more than one child, but I knew I could not afford more than one. That's really not so hard to figure out.

Well, now the Bonker daughter was pregnant. She was nineteen or twenty years old, had never finished high school, was not very bright, and weighed at least three-hundred pounds. She certainly would have had sex with any man who would show her one ounce of attention. There were plenty of dumb drunks who would have sex indiscriminately. That's one of our country's biggest problems.

I was not sure how the Bonkers supported themselves. They had put a taxi sign up on top of their car. Their home was a hovel (right in our downtown) with substandard building methods used. Our winters here were frigid, so I cannot imagine the amount of energy wasted to keep their house warm.

The mother weighed at least three-hundred pounds, the son at least three-hundred, and the dad, well I'd say four-hundred. His stomach hung down to his knees.

Of course these not very bright, morbidly obese people are always shocked when their doctors tell them they have high cholesterol, high blood pressure, or diabetes. They will come in the library looking for books on these health issues. I ask them if their doctors told them they needed to exercise. They always say no. I'm sure the doctors told them, but exercising is as far away from their realities as is eating a healthy diet. These populations really do eat like the personalities from the film, *Fargo,* with huge portions of starchy, fatty foods. They are still consuming fried food on a daily basis, white bread, donuts, and always, always canned fruit and vegetables over fresh, iceberg lettuce loaded with Thousand Island dressing, things that most of us gave up in the sixties or seventies when we started becoming aware of better alternatives.

We are the ones who will pay for all their health problems, since, surely, these families are on lifetime Medicaid. We will pay for the daughter's pregnancy, delivery, and the raising of her child. And to top it all off, this girl smokes and is continuing to smoke while pregnant.

I would like to see pregnant women who smoke or drink or drug arrested and placed in jail to be taken care of while they are pregnant and to keep them from smoking, drinking, or drugging. We will end up paying for the effects of this abuse of their children. The quality of life for the children can be severely damaged as a result of the mothers' lifestyles. That's the saddest part, that so many of these kids will not stand a chance at a decent life.

Chapter Ten
Craziest of the Crazy Mothers

One day a woman came into the library in a rage. She had a torn-up book in a Wal-Mart plastic bag. The book was Tim Allen's *Don't Stand Next to a Naked Man*, a totally harmless book. The woman went ballistic, not wanting her twenty-six year-old daughter reading it. The twenty-six-year-old, still living with her crazy mother, was a product of her Mom, not able to live on her own, both, no doubt, on disability because of mental illness. She had shredded the book by hand in her fury. She came in apologizing, letting us know she just went crazy when she saw her daughter reading this. It might not sound that funny to you as you are reading this, since you can't see these women. For this woman to think a Tim Allen book was going to do her daughter harm after the harm the mother had already inflicted upon her just by parenting her was totally bizarre. I will try to describe her.

She was large with oily, bad skin, short, stringy brown hair. She wore multiple layers of long skirts and tunics. She had a sharp nose, those crazy-looking beady eyes, and squeaky voice.

Her poor daughter was another one who didn't stand a chance at a normal life. She hung out with a man who was a pervert himself. He might be on the criminal-sex-offender list. But for her, this was the absolute best she could expect of life, and they would more than likely have kids who they will ruin.

Super-crazy mom also tended to experiment with religious groups. She had, at one time, been a turbo-Baptist and at one time a turbo-Catholic. Her most recent conversion was into Islam. Yes, this crazy woman had become a Muslim. She showed up at the library in full costume, complete with burka, signed up for a computer, and went straight to a Muslim-terrorist site. When I walked by her I noticed pictures of the 9/11 attackers. This was taking place within a year of the 9/11 attacks. Crazy Mother was corresponding with terrorists when I walked by, and I saw pictures of Atta, one of the terrorists. This seriously alarmed me, since she was the type of mental case who has the luxury of American citizenship, so, many terrorist would love to marry her. It would be their ticket to America. She was printing off a lot of documents. The printer is at the front desk, so we have access to what people are printing. I took a look at her print jobs. They were all filled with documents regarding American-sponsored atrocities in the Middle East. This type of information does not need to be in the hands of crazy, very needy woman.

I let my director know. He wasn't too concerned. She continued to print more and more radical documents. Finally I told my director that if he didn't call the police I would. He called. I felt like she might possibly need to be monitored. I don't know if she had a social worker she checked in with now and then, but someone needed to be aware of what she was involved in before she brought harm to herself or others. Crazy, needy, and vulnerable are not a good combination.

She had only been into the library once or twice since then, but she did not have her burka and Muslim attire on. Who knows what her next metamorphosis would be.

Chapter Eleven
Horny Old Men

When you go to your local library are you aware of any horny old men gathered there? Take a look around. I bet they are lurking there somewhere. Maybe they have a newspaper or magazine resting on their laps covering their lechery. Some may be in a corner looking at a woman, rubbing himself, like the next pervert you're about to meet.

Otto was seventy or so years old and widowed, like so many of our library patrons, and he came into the library, seemingly to read the paper.

Otto had always been overly friendly with me, but I learned to set boundaries with him. A female librarian really can't be friendly with some people without them stepping over the boundaries.

As I have mentioned previously, I am the employee whose workspace is out on the floor of our library, so I see everyone and everything that goes on.

The first complaint I received about Otto came from a thirty-something-year-old woman. She came over to my desk to tell me that he was making her extremely uncomfortable, that he was rubbing himself while looking at her. Whenever she looked up from her reading, he was looking at her and rubbing himself. She couldn't tell if his pants were unzipped.

I told her I would let my director know, which I did immediately after she left. I told her it would be better if she talked to my director, but she didn't want to make that big a deal over it, a pretty typical response from most people. They choose not to tell the manager or director and then just never come back. I think we "normal" people are so used to our concerns and complaints being minimized in favor of the pervert or victimizer or perpetrator that we just don't bother to put forth the effort to complain or voice our concerns. Plus, there is this Disneyland type of forced belief that if we just tolerate anything then it becomes tolerable, that if we just smile and are positive everything will turn out okay.

Once again I have to reiterate something John Bradshaw says: that we're still living under the sickening platitudes from the 1950s, like when Bambi's friend Thumper gets reprimanded by his father when he says something "bad" (but true) about someone, and his father tells him, "If you don't have anything nice to say, don't say anything."

We are "uncomfortable" voicing anything "negative" about someone since we might not recognize, "there but for the grace of God go I" or appear "too closed minded" or "unaware of how lucky we have it" or "not accepting of others as they are."

So I told my director about Otto, and once again he couldn't do anything unless the patron came and said something to him. I don't understand this line of thinking. What does my director think? I am making this up? Why would I make something like this up? Why is the victim the one who has to risk being disregarded? Why couldn't I be considered her advocate? I work there; I see what's going on, and my director doesn't.

Why is my word totally disregarded? We see this attitude in our public schools about bullying. A child will get beaten up. Five or six kids will come forward to tell the administration, but unless the kid (the victim) himself comes forward, no one will do anything about it. We all know if the victim comes forward, he will get a real ass kicking the next day, and still the administration will not do anything.

So farther on down the line, Otto is back, rubbing himself while looking at high-school girls studying. These are high-school girls. Would any one of us have gone and told the director of a library that we felt uncomfortable being there because an elderly adult male (who happens to be the same age as our grandpas) was rubbing himself? Hell no! I would have gotten up and left, feeling violated but not understanding why, just feeling dirty and insecure coming from a place where I should feel secure, a library. These girls have never been back to study. Studying is supposed to be one of the primary purposes of a library, not Internet access for every pervert in town to use. As a matter of fact, we rarely have teens come in to study anymore. They tell me there are too many weirdos, and it's too loud. I agree.

So I once again told my director that Otto was exhibiting the same behavior, and once again I got the same response.

Let me say here that I agree that there are times when the best way to handle a problem is to do nothing, but I don't think that method applies when someone is being victimized. The next Otto episode does not end without consequences.

I normally work on Wednesdays from twelve to eight at night. On this particular Wednesday, I came in at five instead, so most of the day had passed. My director left at about five-thirty. At about five-forty, a grandpa and his twelve-year-old adolescent granddaughter came to the desk, clearly upset. The girl was crying, and the grandfather was trying to speak for her. Between the two of them, I was told that a man had been following her around all day at the library. She had been told by either her parents or grandparents to come to the library and stay all day and not to leave. She was there with some of her friends. We had never had any type of similar complaint or problem with these girls. They come to the library often. She told me that a man had been following her around and rubbing himself. She said she had hidden under a table in the library to try and get away from him or to make him think she had left, but he didn't leave the library. While she was telling me this, I became angry and disgusted. Here this adolescent girl was in a library, with at least six adults working, and not one noticed what was going on with her. Not one person was tuned into what was going on in the library enough to know a little girl was in distress, or that a grown man was making sexual overtures to a minor. I can walk into a room, and within moments, if there is a pervert, child molester, or anyone with criminal tendencies, recognize it within ten minutes. It's in the air around them.

And of course I knew exactly who they were talking about. I asked the girl if the man was still here. She said she thought so. I walked around the library to see who was there, and of course there was Otto hiding in a corner. I asked the girl to walk over near where he was sitting and see if that was the man. She said it was. I told the grandpa, "I'm not surprised. We have had trouble with him before."

I asked the grandpa to write down what had happened, and told him I would give the note to my director. He said he couldn't and told the granddaughter to write it. So she described as best as a twelve-year-old could what had occurred. I included a note telling my director what had happened. I told the girl to be sure and leave her name and phone number. Now, this was on Wednesday. I never, ever considered that my director wouldn't call the girl's parents or grandparents immediately if not sooner the next day. This girl had been sexually pursued in the library by an adult! Well, he didn't call. The mother called the library on Friday, totally freaked out, understandably, yelling at the assistant director. The mother was especially upset that no one had bothered to call her. She asked why nothing had been done about Otto, since we had had problems with him before. I don't know exactly what else was spoken. My assistant director called me into her office and let me have if for telling the grandfather that we'd had problems with Otto before. I told her that if Otto had been dealt with properly the first time, this little girl would not have been victimized and that I was not going to act as though this was the first time we'd had problems. In other words, I was not going to play the everything-is-all-right game. And I said I wasn't going to be yelled at or reprimanded by her when I had done nothing wrong and that their unwillingness to deal with Otto properly had caused a twelve-year-old girl to be victimized. I started to become the cause of this situation. I let them know I had done nothing wrong, that I had tried twice in the past to get them to deal with Otto by relaying to them what had happened to the others with no results at all, that because of their passivity, both the girl and I had been put in situations we shouldn't have had to face.

My director called me from home that night while I was at work, after he heard what had happened. He said to me that I had put him in an awkward situation, especially since we were starting a fund-raising campaign in an effort to add on to the library. My response was, "I put you in an awkward situation? I think you put me and a twelve-year-old girl in a very awkward situation."

The whole thing was a mess. I'm sure if it had been the child or grandchild of a prominent businessman or doctor, they would have sued the library. The parents of this little girl were placated by whatever they were told by our director and assistant director, and everything was hushed up.

Otto was told not to be in the library if this particular little girl was in the library, and not to get within ten feet of a kid, and not to go in the children's section. It was decided that Otto, the pedophile, should monitor himself.

Otto came in once and was told to leave. He went out the back door and then re-entered through the front door and went straight into the children's section.

Another time Otto came in when we had summer reading for kids going on, so the kids' reading sheets were out where everyone had access to them. He started going through the sheets and writing down kids' phone numbers. I don't know if he called any kids. This information was told to me by a fellow employee, since I'm sure my director didn't want me to know about Otto's recent perverted efforts.

I also thought it strange when the assistant director tried to gather information about Otto from the other women who work here, none of whom even knew who Otto was. They didn't know his name or recognize him, since these women are in the back and mostly oblivious to what's going on with our patrons. If they hadn't noticed a twelve-year-old girl trying to escape from Otto all day, I doubt any observations they had would be meaningful. I've seen this happen in other areas where a person in authority wants to hear a chain of events told from a certain perspective, so they keep going from one employee or person to another until they find someone who is willing to go along with what the person in authority wants to hear, and then that story becomes the gospel truth, and the person who was actually there and knows what really happened becomes the outcast, the bad guy, or the person with a negative attitude. We see it happening every day in the political arena. We see it in the corporate world in the way whistle blowers are treated with contempt for speaking the truth. It has become so commonplace we don't even blink an eye when it occurs. I think employers tend to hire malleable, somewhat mercenary individuals with this in mind. A manipulated reality looks better to taxpayers, board members, and stockholders than actual reality.

I was called in to talk with both my supervisors. I was told that my assistant director had concluded that Otto had Alzheimer's (the new catch all illness for all horny old men) and she told me about Otto not being allowed on the premises when kids are here. I don't think half of our staff would recognize Otto if he walked into the library. My director told me that it seemed I disapproved of the way he had handled Otto in the past. Since there had not been any handling, I really did not know what to say. Next time anything like this happens, I will definitely call the police, which is what I wish I had done when this incident first happened.

Chapter Twelve
Wall of Bums

We have a wall of bums at our library. On any given day I can glance into our reading area and see four to ten men, ranging in age from mid-twenties to sixty. Some days these men will sit in the library from opening to closing. Rarely do they read. They sit there and sometimes talk with each other, but more often they try to engage other library patrons, who are strangers. Does anything annoy you more than going out to accomplish one of your many errands (especially when you're in a hurry which most of us are) and someone who apparently has nothing else to do decides he can just start talking with you, expecting a response? I have little discretionary time, and what I do have I don't want to spend talking with someone who had made a choice to be a lonely shell of a person. I feel violated when someone just assumes I want to talk with them, especially a person who has nothing more interesting to say than where they plan to go for their next free meal.

The highlight of the bums' conversation is what church or senior center will offer them their next meal. What happened to pride? What happened to self- reliance? These men don't seem embarrassed by the fact that they don't have anyone to have dinner with besides strangers. These men have enough money to feed themselves. We all know it doesn't take much to feed one person. A loaf of bread, some peanut butter and jelly, and you're set for a week or so. Instead, these guys rely on churches that put a lot of pressure on their congregations to provide meals for them. Sorry, but my husband and I work full time and do whatever we have to do to provide for our three kids and some of our extended families. We both worked hard and made difficult choices to get to a point where we could afford to have children and care for them as well.

For those of us in service, a library worker and teacher, we give to people all day for very little money. I see people who have made dumb decisions all day long. Their stupid decisions cause immeasurable pain for their children and society as a whole.

Several on the wall are burnt-out alcoholics on disability. Why would someone who chooses to continue to drink receive disability? I know alcoholism is a very serious disease. I have alcoholism running rampant in my family. But there is so much help available now for all addictions, there is no excuse for letting these illnesses take over a whole life. Several of the wall bums are men in their late twenties or early thirties who sit in the library all day, either staring into space or playing computer games. Do we really want to support this?

What happened to the human characteristic that pushes people to provide for themselves, especially men? These men are totally without this drive. They don't seem to feel any humiliation or shame about being parasites.

One of the alcoholics lives at the hotel across the street. The others appear to have their own homes. Several of the younger men still live with their mothers! One of the bums was broadcasting that his son had received a full scholarship to the same state university that my son attends. He is receiving this scholarship because of his parents' lack of income. These are the times when I wish I'd just chosen to be a bum. His kid is getting a full scholarship because his parents made stupid decisions.

I used to hear people say we rewarded people for doing nothing, and I thought, *Well, there aren't that many people who need help*. I thought no one would chose dependence over independence if he had a choice. I was wrong. They were right. And sometimes I wonder, from an evolutionary standpoint, why is it that the mentally incompetent are thriving, but the mentally competent aren't? Families and individuals with higher incomes and advanced education are having fewer children, but since they tend to live in ivory-tower areas of the country, they don't see what is occurring in our population.

Is our population devolving instead of evolving?

Chapter Thirteen
The Yucks

The Yucks are a family of four with mental deficiencies resulting from inbreeding. They have the same facial asymmetry as the Appalachians depicted in the film, *Deliverance*. You know the look I'm talking about: the inbred look. Between the four of them, the IQ might total one-hundred.

The Yucks live on an in-town stretch of highway. Their empire of rusted vehicles, sheet metal, cinder blocks, and God knows what else is enclosed by a sheet-metal fence. The junkyard homestead goes on for about a quarter mile, but every so often, there is a gap, so a driver or passenger can get a glimpse of their collection, a quarter mile of rusted-metal monoliths.

They only used the computers when they came into the library. I doubt reading was an activity they engaged in often.

Well, one day I saw in the paper that the Yucks had been

arrested for possession of a U.S. Government-issue, hand-held missile launcher. So I guess they were searching the Internet for artillery for starting a third world war.

What a sense of security that brings me; how about you?

Chapter Fourteen
Leeanne

Leeanne was a grown woman who was very mentally impaired. She was a ward of the state since she didn't have any family left living, and her family did not provide for their impaired child, so the taxpayers got to shoulder this expense.

Sadly, no one wanted to be with Leeanne, not even her state-appointed guardian who was paid to spend some time with her. Leeanne was really annoying. She repeated herself over and over again with a nasally squeaky voice. She would constantly ask if you had missed her. She was very desperate for attention.

Unlike most of the other library patrons I've introduced you to, Leeanne was pretty harmless. Fortunately, she had not reproduced, so she would not be responsible for parenting a child. She had several times tried to find the phone numbers of children who visit the library. I suppose, since she had the IQ of a child, that was why she tried to develop relationships with them, but this did not go over well with the parents of the kids she called. I don't blame the parents at all for being concerned and alarmed over a mentally impaired older woman calling their children.

Leeanne walked around town with two large, purple, Barney stuffed animals. She took our town's local Dial-A-Ride. Those of you living in big cities will not believe how our public transportation operates. We have at least four large buses equipped with handicap lifts in our Dial-A-Ride fleet. There is not a set schedule whereby the rider waits for the bus. No, the rider calls for the bus, and the bus comes to get him. I know you are as shocked to read this as I was to discover it upon moving here. There isn't any thought of efficiency at all. There are rarely more than three people, at the most, on a bus. The individuals who use these buses, for the most part, are handicapped people on disability who have no schedules at all. They could easily accommodate the buses' set schedule instead of the bus accommodating theirs. Leeanne was one person who used this service. She would take Dial-A-Ride from her house, which was in town, to the library, also in town, and then would call the bus again to leave the library and go two blocks, and then after she took care of her business, she called them again. I asked her why she didn't walk, especially when it was a lovely day out, and she said she did not want to or that her hat might blow off.

The State of Michigan's economy is the worst in the country

right now, and yet the State of Michigan provides hundreds of thousands of dollars for this inefficient public transportation. This year, the State of Michigan will be contributing another two hundred thousand dollars to our Dial-A-Ride so they can purchase another bus. Why not purchase a Volkswagen or some other vehicle with great fuel economy?

At the same time, our public school teachers haven't had raises in three years, and there is no money for textbooks, but more money goes each year for at-risk and special-education kids. Our gifted-and-talented kids are being dragged down and bored to tears in classes where teachers are stuck with the task of bringing all the low-achieving kids to passing levels so these kids can pass the qualifications for the No Child Left Behind mess.

Leeanne's own guardian did not let Leeanne have her phone number, since Leeanne would call her constantly. Leeanne was terrified of lightning and thunder. She would call us at the library several times any day when the weather looked threatening. We started having her call the police, although I'm not really sure what they were authorized to do for her.

Leeanne is in her fifties now. Physically, she appears to be fine. She could go on living quite a long time. She, thank goodness, is retarded enough to have never had to try to fit into any type of public school setting or any other place where the people have average IQs. Hopefully she is not fully aware of how unwanted and uncared for she is.

She does still pine away for a boyfriend. She settles for a repulsive, cruel, retarded man who treats her terribly. This is the best she can expect of life.

Chapter Fifteen
Beth

Beth was another mentally handicapped adult woman. Everyone else in her family was mentally impaired; all were on disability, including the mother. Beth was old enough to live away from home, but her mother wanted the disability check, so Beth was kept under her mother's control, even though her mother hadn't done anything to enrich Beth's life.

Beth came into the library to use our computers. She was obsessed with Mariah Carey and several other shapely, famous women. She made color copies of these women and kept them in a notebook. I'm sure that if she had access to the cities in which they live, she would stalk them.

Beth went through our public school system as an inclusion-special-education student. Are you aware that for some of the special-education students, the schools are required by federal law to hire a teacher or teacher's aid for one kid? Now keep in mind that our average and above-average kids don't get much, if any, help at all, but our school system is required by law to give some special-education kids their own teacher. I noticed in my son's high school yearbook that our high school/junior high school complex had thirteen special education teachers and aids. Thirteen special education teachers or aids in a school district that graduates one hundred fifty to two hundred seniors a year. When I was a senior in high school some thirty years ago, we had one special education teacher. Why do we need so many now? Why are there so many special education kids? Some of it is environmental, but most of it is poor choices by the parents. No one seems to be comfortable talking about these issues, even though it affects all of us.

Beth is not living a happy life. She has been placed in several jobs where she has been dismissed for stealing. When a human doesn't have the brain capacity to think as a human to function in her environment, we really don't have a human being.

I'm always perplexed when I hear the courts calling in experts to determine if a murderer or rapist is sane enough to stand trial for his or her crimes. Well, of course they aren't sane. Sane people don't murder, rape, molest, or harm helpless children or animals.

While working at the library, I can determine which kids will grow up to be criminals by the time they are eight or ten years old. When they can't function in the society they are expected to function in, and there is no one there to take care of them, a life of crime is the only option. They simply can't make it any other way.

Beth's mom always has some new skanky, drunkard boyfriend who is more important to her than Beth. Often, she or the boyfriend will be late picking Beth up from the library. One winter night Beth's mom was three hours late picking her up. I had to stay at the library with her. Her mom had told her to never get a ride home with anyone else. I am sure the mom is concealing a lot about their lives to keep all the entitlement benefits coming to her. I would have given her a ride happily, but instead, we waited as the snow fell. After two hours, I called the police. I felt this was neglectful of the mom and should be reported to social services. The first thing Beth asked when the officer came in was if the officer was married. No matter how impaired a human being is, the sex drive remains intact. This is especially true among mentally handicapped males, sadly. After clearing up everyone's marital status, the officer took all the necessary information from Beth. This all took another hour or so. The officer was just about ready to give Beth a ride home when, who should show up, but a partially sober, skanky boyfriend, who had obviously just awoken. He had forgotten to wake up and get Beth. He was all worked up about the policeman being there. He just couldn't quite grasp that the policeman was there because of his neglect. He kept saying that we didn't need to do that and other nonsense. Beth, of course, chose to ride home with the skanky boyfriend.

The next day the mother called the library wanting to know who had called the police and why. The officer had done his job and reported the incident to social services. Social services contacted the mother. They probably had made some inquiries or perhaps even made a visit to the home. So the mother felt the proper response was for her to be furious. Narcissism seems to run hand in hand with craziness in some people. She could only see how this affected her; how it threatened to take away the money she was receiving from the state and federal government for the care of Beth. She did not have the intellectual capacity to evaluate her behavior, so she would never be able to change it. With her low IQ, she was not able to realize how inappropriate her behavior was, so there is no chance for positive change.

So the mom called the library wanting to know who and why the police were called. No apologies were offered for making the library staff person wait three hours for her child to be picked up, no remorse nor regret was felt for neglecting her child or leaving her in the care of an irresponsible lout of a boyfriend.

There is one household in town that I know of that has a teenage daughter with two handicapped children. The mother encouraged the daughter to drink while she was pregnant, since she would get more money for a handicapped child. For those of us who take parenting seriously, this mind set is too crazy to believe, but please, believe it. These adults do not seem to have the capacity to love their children. They cannot support themselves, so having kids and handicapping them to get more money somehow becomes a viable option to them. Their children's well being is completely inconsequential.

Chapter Sixteen
Garden-Variety Drunks and Crazies

Conan—Conan was an adult-male drunk. He had been in and out of treatment, jail, rehab, and Twelve-Step programs. Alcoholism had a terribly strong hold on him. I have watched him deteriorate for years.

Conan had several times brought in books that were destroyed. When I would point it out to him he would simply shrug his shoulders and say, "So?" I would point out to him that normally he didn't bring back our books in this condition. I asked him why he would destroy the books and sometimes he would start yelling something like, he simply felt like it and for me to stop harassing him.

Harold—Harold was another adult-male drunk whose experiences with alcohol were similar to Conan's. Harold brought books back with beer spilled on them quite frequently. Once when I pointed this out to him, his response was that he was a regular patron here, so it seems like I would treat him better and show him some respect, as if the library would cease to exist without his presence. Certainly this person did not contribute financially to the library, since he was a drunken bum who spent a significant amount of his life in jail soaking up thousands of dollars in our criminal justice system. But he viewed himself as a valuable library patron instead of as a drunken parasite.

The Stems—The Stems are another family who, between the two boys, mom, and dad had a combined IQ of around one hundred. I'd been told that the dad spends his time roller skating at our local rink. The boys are both dim-witted, with high testosterone levels. They both have "Destined to be a sexual predator," written all over them.

One day Rufus, one of the boys, came into the library with a young girl. Rufus isn't allowed to use our computers since he was caught on pornographic sites, nor is he permitted to check out books, since he has large fines. The young girl who was with him wanted to sign up for a library card. If a person is under eighteen, their parents or legal guardians, have to sign them up, since the parent or guardian would be responsible for making sure all items were returned. This young girl was only fifteen. She told me she was an emancipated minor and that Rufus was her legal guardian, since he was her husband. She also had a baby who Rufus, with his

IQ of probably at eighty at the highest, was now the legal father. I told them we would need legal proof of this from the courthouse, so they went over there and got the documents. Her parents had, first of all, allowed their fifteen-year-old daughter to become pregnant, have a baby, and become emancipated, and they had given guardianship of their daughter and grand child to an idiot with a high, predatory, sex drive. What a lovely scenario.

We see many women with very little going for them and very few options in life marrying men with criminal sexual-conduct records and having children with them.

Should a person who has engaged in inappropriate sexual acts with children ever be allowed out of jail, much less be allowed to have children?

I think we just pretend not to notice these terribly unfortunate situations. Maybe you think they don't affect you, so why bother? Maybe you think God will watch over and protect these children. God doesn't. These sexual predators are everywhere, along with the insane parents who raised them.

The Naked Patron—This was told to me by one of my co-workers. I didn't see it myself, but I know this person would not make up something like this.

One night my co-worker was closing up the library. We stay open until eight o'clock three nights a week. We also have three separate private rooms patrons can use for studying, playing chess, having meetings, or using a typewriter.

This incident occurred before we had computers, so we had quite a few requests to use our typewriter.

Turning out lights, the employee was checking each private room, making sure no patrons were still inside. He came upon a completely naked patron sitting at the typewriter. This patron had made himself completely at home.

Every day those of us working at the library find ourselves saying, "What is wrong with these people?"

Chapter Seventeen
Strychnine

Here in the rural Midwest a lot of older men wear those denim-type overalls (hogwashers) sometimes with the bottoms unbuttoned on both sides. The lack of pride or inhibition when it comes to how they look never ceases to amaze me.

One day while I was speaking with a gathering of female library patrons, a large older man with his overalls on and unbuttoned stood alongside the gathering of women at my desk. I know him as a weirdo library patron. There were three or four other staff members available at the front desk, but instead, he stood on the outskirts of the group waiting to speak with me. So we paused in our conversation so he could make his inquiry. He asked me if I knew where he could get some strychnine. Suddenly everyone around me became still and quiet. I could see them wondering, what kind of arrangement I might have with this wiry, gray-haired, burly-looking beast of a man desperately seeking out his strychnine connection. For some reason the weirdos with the bizarre questions seek me out. My son tells me there is something in my eyes that makes people feel comfortable talking with me about anything. One of my many nicknames in high school was Barbara Walters (or Wa-Wa as we used to say to mimic her famous speech impediment). I really did not know how to respond. I simply said, "No, I don't really know." He went on to tell me he needed it to get rid of some rodents, but I had to wonder why he came all the way over to my desk and waited at least ten minutes when he could have asked any of the other three staff members.

This man was part of a perplexingly sad, strange family whose mental deficiencies I can't quite pinpoint. They were the types of people who have some sort of personality disorder or who were just raised in such a backwoods, oppressed environment that they could not fit in nor function as productive members of society. An employer/employee relationship would be difficult if not impossible for him or his wife. They might be able to work in factories, but even then, workers have to listen to authority, be somewhat rational, and somewhat emotionally stable, and be able to sometimes get along with others.

This couple came in from way out in the boondocks and checked out tons of books. I don't know how they lived financially; there may have been some kind of family trust fund or they may have be on disability. They had a daughter who was murdered by her husband.

Since living here, I have met three parents who have had a child murdered. All the other places I had lived, I had never met a family who had a child murdered. I've known many families who have lost a child to suicide, car accidents, or cancer, but not murder.

In two of the families, the daughters married crazy men who, as it turned out, had murdered previous wives and had not been caught or were found not guilty because of insufficient evidence. I realize many of the rapists and murderers walking around appear to be perfectly charming on the surface, and that most sociopaths live in neighborhoods and hold down jobs. But in this case, the mom, in all her craziness, had sensed that there was something sinister about her daughter's husband. The daughter did not possess the ability to discern a good person from a bad person. She lacked the antennae we all need to function safely in social situations. We all need to be able to recognize when a person is invading our space or not acknowledging boundaries. I do not see this awareness in families where the kids are neglected. They are perfectly comfortable with whoever is with them. There is no awareness that a person's behavior might be odd. There is a perfect lack of self-consciousness or self awareness.

This couple only knew me from the library, yet they told me the whole tragic story of their daughter meeting this man (who had two previous wives, one missing and never found) marrying him, and shortly afterwards, turning up missing. The husband was a suspect, but once again there was not enough evidence to charge him until some kind of break came along a year or so afterwards, and they were able to press charges. He was found guilty and told where their daughter's body was. He was given life in prison.

This is the kind of stuff we read about in the papers but hope never happens to us or anyone we know. While working at the public library, I've met people who have been affected by the criminally insane who are running loose among us.

Chapter Eighteen
Genealogy

Across the street from our library is a housing complex for the elderly. This isn't one of those upscale, private retirement communities. The Towers (as they are called) offers housing on a sliding-scale basis for moderate-to-low-income elderly. The apartments remain full at all times, since the population in this county is mostly blue-collar, middle-to-low income. So of course, a lot of our patrons live in the Towers.

For reasons to which I absolutely cannot relate, a lot of these folks (many my age and even younger) are obsessed with genealogy. They must think they are going to come upon a king or duke among their family, even though most people who migrated from Europe were poor, landless peasants.

But the part that really gets me is that they imagine I might care to hear about their genealogies. It's as if their egos have gone out of control to such a degree that they think everyone is interested in their families. Hey, I have my own family whose genealogy I hardly concern myself with, so I certainly don't care about someone else's. What makes anyone think that a complete stranger would want to hear about his or her genealogy? It's as if these seekers cannot stand coming to terms with how insignificant they are, so they search around for something significant in their genealogy.

This one particular woman from the Towers would bring over pictures from the past to have them copied. She started becoming a regular, daily patron. She happened to have very large breasts that sagged down to her thighs, which she didn't bother trying to contain in a bra any longer. So they were pretty much an entity of their own. She had wild white hair, a loud voice, and that particular wired, crazy look. As she became a daily patron, she began talking to me about being a widow and how she'd like a man. (Once again our libidos live on!) She started feeling comfortable enough to just walk up to a group of men sitting at a table reading their newspapers and asking who among them was married. I only wish such a lack of subtlety and subterfuge had been acceptable back when I was out searching for a fine man, having to pretend I wasn't searching. She (sadly, I have forgotten her name) would sit down with the group on her own invitation and lead them in conversation. After thirty minutes or so I would hear her evaluation of these men. Usually it would consist of, "Shut up. You don't got nothing to say. Let him talk." I just loved how it would only take her thirty minutes to decide who was full of bullshit and who wasn't, fairly discerning for an eighty-nine-year-old, large-breasted woman, who had led me to believe she could only talk about genealogy.

You'll remember several years ago there were shootings on the Ohio turnpike. Some crazy person was shooting motorists from a bridge that crossed the turnpike. This really had no repercussions for our town except for the sadness we all felt for the victims and their families, and yes, something like that could happen anywhere, but I don't think many residents here felt threatened.

Well, one day she came walking into the library and stopped right in the middle of the doorway, oblivious to the fact that she was blocking everyone trying to go in or out. She yelled in her loudest voice, hands on her hips, breasts flapping, "Well, we're all safe to go back in the streets now. They've caught the shooter." I had not heard the news but figured out what she was talking about. She went up to just about everyone to let them know the shooter had been caught. She was letting us all know it was safe to go back out into the streets, as though we had confined ourselves to our homes those past months or stayed away from the streets.

Chapter Nineteen
Millennium

You would not believe the number of phone calls we received at the library at the millennium (1999-2000), from people wondering where the highest point in Michigan was. It seems all the Michigan Militia and survivalists were heading to the highest points to be prepared for any number of natural disasters. I thought it was somewhat peculiar that a survivalist or militia member wouldn't already know any and all facts regarding Michigan terrain. I don't know how many people actually packed up and headed for the hills, but I'm sure quite a few did. I'm sure the Yucks wished they'd had their hand-held rocket launcher.

You simply would not believe the reference calls and questions we receive at the library, not just at the Millennium. A lot of, "How do you spell this word?" even though anyone can purchase a dictionary for less than ten dollars or for a dollar at a yard sale, questions normal people should be embarrassed to ask. We have at our disposal encyclopedias, dictionaries, and the Internet, yet people would rather call us and ask.

Another amazing finding is how many educated people do not know how to use a library. I don't think a person should be awarded a teaching certificate if he can't find something in a library. I have had an elementary art teacher come into the library after reading *The DaVinci Code*, wanting information about DaVinci. While I was helping her find books about DaVinci, she told me she wasn't familiar with DaVinci and that she not only couldn't identify his paintings, but didn't know he had such a large body of work.

On a regular basis, I have teachers come into the library raving over a Danielle Steele novel. I have heard of teachers assigning Danielle Steele, or other pop-fiction novels as possible choices on a reading list. I don't want my kids taught by teachers who think that Danielle Steele or any other mainstream writer, with some but very few exceptions, is an appropriate selection on an English-class reading list.

When hiring teachers the interviewer should ask what they read for enjoyment. When hiring a minister ask what they read for inspiration. If it's Erma Bombeck or Peanuts, don't hire them. What a person reads says a lot about what type of person he is and what he cares about and values. It can indicate a person of substance versus a person of fluff. Why would an adult want to spend hours of his or her day reading fluff on a regular basis unless he chooses to be unaware? It's as if we try not to improve ourselves. There are plenty of novels that require brain power to read, but they are not regularly checked out of the library. If we only had what was popular at the library, our library would be an intellectual void.

I know teachers are not paid much, so we aren't going to get the brainiest of students in education. This needs to be completely overhauled. We need to attract the best and brightest by paying them well and making education programs more rigorous.

Chapter Twenty
Lying Patrons

Since we all learned in third grade about how our town, city, and county governments run, we know that public libraries are generally financed by the taxpayers living in the town, city, or county. The only monetary payment requirement we have is for a person to either reside in the county or, if they don't, pay a very small yearly fee to use the library. The fee is nowhere near the taxed amount a resident pays for the library. For a very small fee, a person is given access to thousands of books, magazines, DVDs, CDs, books on cassettes and CDs, and computers.

Even though the fee is small and very fair, there was one family who used our library but chose to lie about their residence. This family also happened to be turbo, fundamentalist Christian. I would say surprisingly, but I have noticed that the turbo-Christian population in our town seems to lie more than other populations.

They seem to believe that since they are doing "the Lord's work," it's okay for them to lie. Of course they aren't doing the Lord's work. This particular family had two of the most screwed-up kids I have ever met. The kids are adults now, and they are not on speaking terms with their parents, nor can either child fit into any group or niche. These kids remind me of the mixed-up chameleon in Eric Carle's children's book.

I have noticed that a number of the kids who are home schooled or from turbo-Christian, fundamentalist families are odd. They are frequently loners and only seem to feel comfortable in their church groups. There are several single mothers in our community who are home schooling their boys. I have watched them over the years at the library, and these boys are social misfits. I fear the types of relationships they are drawn to frequently end up being the ones heard about on the news: "He was such a quiet guy." "We never thought he would do anything like that." "He mostly kept to himself." Have you ever taken a look at the textbooks some of the Christian home schooling families are using? Take a look sometime. Their texts are written from a biblical perspective. I realize none of us can know absolutely what has occurred historically, but we do have a fairly accurate idea (of course from the victors).

The parents who lied about their residence were found out, and when we asked them about it, they pretended they didn't understand our question. They had their little, "What would Jesus do?" bands on their wrists. I see a lot of CEOs and business owners wearing these bracelets as they lay off workers or cut their insurance benefits instead of lessening their own huge salaries and benefit packages.

My husband, who is a high-school English teacher, has turbo-Christian kids in his classes who are not comfortable seeing pictures of great art where there is a breast, derriere, or penis visible, or reading a poetic work that has sexual imagery, sexual themes, or even words regarding the body. But they never seem to mind gratuitous violence, and are completely unconcerned about the environment or endangered species, and maintain that the planet is here for human consumption. They will excuse themselves from the classroom when offended, sometimes complaining to their parents or the principal.

I recognize that there are some parents who home school their kids and do a great job. They have well adjusted, balanced kids, but at the library I mostly see the parents whose greatest gift would be to allow their children to go to school.

Chapter Twenty-One
Leon

Leon was eighty or so years old. He and his brother both had very odd speech patterns, and I have wanted to tape them and send the tape to an anthropologist, linguist, or speech pathologist who could discover how they developed such weird speech patterns. The emphasis was on the wrong part of the word, and the rhythm was all discombobulated.

Leon sometimes arrived at the library on his bike. With some ingenious type of makeshift attachment he'd have junk roped onto both sides of the bike. He rode into town from quite a distance.

Leon and his brother both had major screws loose. Leon was a radical Catholic, who was usually on the Catholic-singles website. Leon talked constantly to anybody. It didn't matter if anyone was listening. Like most compulsive talkers, he talked loudly and never made sense. He liked to try to convert people to Catholicism.

He had a cow with spots on it, and he claimed the placement of the spots formed a picture of the Virgin Mary. He brought in a picture of the cow to show us.

When Leon came in, we tried to place him as far away from people as possible. He generally had a million questions he needed to ask that didn't have answers, so he was constantly coming up to the front desk to ask unanswerable questions.

We have a lot of patrons who ask questions that have no answers. It usually takes the combined skills of Sherlock Holmes and Miss Marple to figure out what some patrons are asking.

Chapter Twenty-Two
The Do-It-Yourself-Divorce (If I Only Had the Brains) Patrons

No lie, some days we'll have up to three people, with or without minor kids, come into the library for the do-it-yourself-divorce book. This is a reference book, so they have to look it over on their own and decide what forms they need to have copied.

Many times the person simply cannot read. Usually, the patron's reading comprehension skills are not good enough to understand the text, and we are not permitted (by law) to help them read it. Plus, divorce is not supposed to be easy. Marriage, parenting, and divorce are not incidental cakewalks we are supposed to take multiple times.

Almost always, the women who come in are dragging around another loser guy with whose child they are already pregnant and who they intend to marry as soon as they figure out how to divorce the loser to whom they are currently married.

They almost always have an entourage with them too: mother, sister, auntie, and maybe several other ex-husbands and various offspring.

What makes these women think the next marriage will be different, or that the next guy will have any redeeming qualities when she hasn't done anything to change, improve, or enhance her self?

Breaking up a marriage should be painful. It should feel like its breaking the heart and soul apart. It's meant to be the most significant relationship in our lives, along with the relationships we have with our children. These women and men have absolutely no concern over the impact this has on their children, either. No matter how well we handle divorce, it is always unsettling for children, but these people treat divorce like it's just the next thing they do.

I want so badly to say, "Girlfriend, this guy is a loser, and you need to work on yourself and find out who you really are and what you really want."

Sometimes, they'll get mad at us for simply not doing it all for them. They want us to find the forms they need and tell them how to fill out each form. It's as though someone has done everything for them so far in their lives, and they don't know how to do anything on their own. Most of these women are still dependent on their very dysfunctional mothers, who seem to be their best friends and more than likely, mom will be moving in with daughter and her new loser husband. Maybe mom will be their in-home child care provider so the daughter and son-in-law can keep going out to bars at night.

This leaves me with a sense of hopelessness. This will go on generation after generation. These men and women yell at their kids and hit them right there in the library, so I cannot imagine what they do to the children at home.

Chapter Twenty-Three
Mr. Magoo

Mr. Magoo is an elderly, crazy, pseudo-intellectual man. He sometimes wears two pairs of glasses, resembling a frog peering through ice.

Mr. Magoo, in his lame attempts to sound intelligent, will verbosely use a string of obscure words in a sentence as simple as, "Can I sign up for a computer?" These sentences never really make sense, even after I have tried to dissect them. One could say he's pretentious, but he's too mentally ill for that.

Mr. Magoo only shows up in the summer time. He appears in May and departs in the autumn. He comes in the library to use our computers. Our policy is that a person can sign up for one hour of computer use a day. Apparently, a library is not permitted to enforce its own policy, since Mr. Magoo simply could not understand why, if there were computers available, he couldn't stay on one as long as he liked. He questioned every single procedure we had. For instance, when we would sign a patron up for the computer he was currently using, he would have a fit, not realizing or caring that all the other computers were reserved, even though the patron who reserved it wasn't actually there yet. He would come up to the front desk, with his pseudo-intellectual psycho babble, to question everything. Now why couldn't we just say, "That's just our policy," and leave it at that? I go many places and encounter policies with which I don't agree. Mr. Magoo always objected, complained, and refused to follow any of our policies. I thought this would be a perfect reason to kick him out of the library. The staff would all have been much happier. He could take his complaints over to the courthouse if he liked. I'm sure they would tell him that the library is allowed to have policies.

Well, one day Mr. Magoo arrived at the library with his own computer. I don't mean a wireless computer that he can access with our wireless connection. No, apparently he had a computer at home all along. Our guess was that he was so annoying that his wife wanted him out of the house, so she would drop him off at the library where he could, hopefully, use our computers all day.

So he showed up with his computer, and our director spent several hours with him getting it set up and operating. He had ongoing questions that used up either our director's time or a workers' time. And at the end of his time at the library, someone had to assist him in dismantling his computer since he didn't know how to do any of it. He repeated this for a week or so. Either his wife figured out it was too much trouble, or my director told him it was too much trouble. Then he was back using our computers and let us know he was trying to realize and understand the limits we set on computer use.

Mr. Magoo also liked to chat with any and everyone in the library. It didn't matter who the person was or what he was doing, he'll start talking with that patron. A student might be trying to do homework, studying for a test, typing a paper, or just wanting not to be bothered; he'd talk to that person anyway.

My desk is set up in the young-adult section of the library. I have kids who, on a regular basis, come in after school and do their homework until their parents pick them up between five and six o'clock. Throughout the school year, I have several kids who come in daily and sit at the same desks daily.

One day Mr. Magoo decided to go over and sit at the same desk as a seventh-grade girl who came in daily. Now remember, Celeste was only in seventh grade, so she was about twelve years old. Mr. Magoo started asking her all kinds of personal questions. He had been talking with her for almost an hour when one of my co-workers came over to me, suggesting that Celeste might need some help getting rid of Mr. Magoo. We were about to head over there to point out to Mr. Magoo that Celeste was trying to do her homework so it might be best if he excused himself. Suddenly it was decided by management that it would be better to remove Celeste from the place where she studies every day, the desk where her mother would expect her to be when she came to get her, the seat where she had me sitting practically next to her.

So we had to go over and ask Celeste to come to the employee area in the back. We told her to bring her books and everything with her. She was surprised and confused. We asked her if Mr. Magoo was bothering her, since we had noticed she couldn't get her homework done, and like a good girl, she said no. We told her it would be better for her to do her homework in back where no one would bother her. We told her Mr. Magoo would assuredly continue to talk to her until it was time for her to go. She felt odd back there with a bunch of adults, strangers. I assured her I would catch her mom when she walked in the door looking for her, and then I would escort her back out into the library.

But as we were taking Celeste away from the desk, Mr. Magoo became agitated and could not comprehend why we were removing Celeste. He started acting offended and outraged that we might be suggesting that he was annoying or harming or bothering her. His sense of self-importance, along with plain-old craziness, just blinded him to the fact that he was a walking annoyance.

I find it wrong that Celeste, a twelve-year-old girl doing homework, was removed from her comfort zone, instead of Mr. Magoo being asked to move to another table. Once again the squeaky wheel got the grease.

It seems the whole world is made afraid and inhibited by any possible retaliation from crazy people and their families. What happened to the rights of the rest of us? If Mr. Magoo's family was going to drop him off at the library for the day, they needed to make sure he kept his craziness under control and didn't bother other people. Dropping him off was like dropping off a two-or three-year-old at the library without a babysitter.

The next day Mr. Magoo came up to me and in a very stern voice started reprimanding me. He told me he was feeling very negative energy, or something of that nature, from me when I came and removed that young girl, and that he hadn't been bothering her.

I wanted to reply to him, "Well, now you know how she felt." Instead I pointed out to him that she was doing her homework and needed to be left alone. He started to make more remarks, so I walked away.

Celeste's mother showed up and was a little panicked. Our assistant director took the mother into her office, and they talked for a while, but Mr. Magoo just went his merry way, seeking out someone else to annoy or seeing if there were some other policies he could overturn.

There was another incident with Mr. Magoo. Celeste was sitting at her usual desk doing her homework after school. Mr. Magoo went right up to her desk, even though there were plenty of other desks available, and proceeded to chat with her. I could tell by the look on Celeste's face that she was in shock. Remember, she was twelve-years-old, and this old guy was talking with her even though it had been forbidden. I instant messaged my assistant director immediately. I was told that it was up to Celeste to let an adult know that Mr. Magoo was bothering her. I hope you, dear reader are just as frustrated and angered by this as I was. And then, when Mr. Magoo finished talking to Celeste, (not "with" but "to") he stopped by my desk, about ten feet from Celeste. He tried to engage me in conversation, but I ignored him. He became agitated by my not responding, but I had nothing nice to say to him. He babbled on about how rude I was being.

I finally simply said, "Mr. Magoo, I am a quiet person." I couldn't say what I wanted to say or what needed to be said. Then, with a sweeping gesture of his hand indicating he meant Celeste, he told me that he intended to have an on-going relationship with this lovely young woman whether I approve of it or not.

When Celeste's dad came, I let him know what had occurred. Of course he was frustrated and angry that no one was protecting his daughter. A twelve-year-old girl is often not going to come to an adult for help in a situation like this, nor should she have to. He asked what he should do about it, and I recommended he go to the board, since the situation wasn't being handled to his satisfaction.

Chapter Twenty-Four
Greedy, Unenlightened Patrons

For reasons beyond my comprehension, an investment group was allowed to meet at the library. Normally only non-profit groups were permitted to reserve one of our available rooms. This group of women was permitted to use one of our rooms on a regular weekly basis to discuss investment possibilities.

One of the women in this group was the current matriarch to one of the more affluent families that has deep roots in Denialville. She and her family were quite well off. I can't guess what their assets are worth, but I am pretty sure she could come up with a dollar. Here is her story of greed at its finest.

The library has an Inter-Library Loan program. This program enables libraries to borrow from other libraries for their patrons, giving libraries a wider selection of books to choose from without having to purchase all of them, especially convenient since there is only so much space on the shelves. Our greedy matriarch put in a request for an investment book. The library requires the patron to pay postage, which is normally one dollar, unless the person is requesting an over-sized book. We are supposed to make the patron aware of this policy when we take the book request so that they know in advance.

When the grand matriarch came in for her inter-library-loan book, she refused to pay the dollar postage. She stated that nobody told her about the postage charge; therefore, she refused to pay on principle. What her principle was I don't really know. I guess it might have been the squeaky wheel gets the grease, or no millionaire left behind, or if one is really stingy with wealth that's okay, since they have worked so hard, and the rest of us have been sitting around in our nightgowns eating bonbons.

Of course, she was allowed to get away with her selfish, unenlightened, psycho behavior.

I continue to log complaints to my director about how ethically wrong it seems to allow an investment group to secure a room in the library, since the rooms are only supposed to be used by non-profit organizations.

The group discontinued meeting at the library finally. They may have simply disbanded on their own, or maybe it occurred to them to meet at someone's home instead.

Chapter Twenty-Five
Book Writers

There have been several patrons who have written books. These books, for the most part, are unreadable.

There is a tremendous obsession with local history in this area. It seems like at least three quarters of the population is either still living in the past or wishes it were living in the past.

This town is located on Lake Michigan. The Merchant Marines were a large presence here long ago. This town has preserved one of the huge vessels used during that time and now uses it to ferry people, with or without their car, to Wisconsin.

It is a nice idea, but unfortunately, the coal-fired engines were not replaced. It wasn't made mandatory to replace them; instead they were grandfathered in. You know the completely insane concept of letting something harmful, bad, or illegal continue since at one time it wasn't considered harmful, bad, or illegal. So every day and all day throughout the spring and summer, there is a huge plume of coal-fired black smoke blowing out of the smokestack of this huge car ferry. They'll call you a negative person if you say anything about the toxicity of the smoke. They'll tell you it wouldn't be cost effective, and that the car ferry would go out of business if it were required to replace the coal-fired engines. I say, so be it. Clean air and a less likely chance of cancer are worth more than a historical car ferry and the jobs it provides. People actually take pictures of it, black smoke and all. Their romanticizing of the elephant in the middle of the living room is appalling.

Two of the male authors have written about the car ferries. One of the authors, Parker, would come in and have us make copies from other books on the history of car ferries and Great Lakes freighters and ships. He was really particular about the size of the text when we made his copies, always wanting us to make tiny adjustments. Sometimes he would demand we redo a page four or five times and not expect to pay for any of the copies. Actually most of our patrons, for some reason, assume copies will be free. Do you know of anywhere where you can expect to get free copies?

Eventually Parker's book came out. All he had done was pretty much rearrange the copies we had made for him, along with retyping some of the information, and there you had his book.

Jameson was the other historian/author. He was also a psycho pervert. He came into the library on just about a daily basis. I'm not sure what was wrong with him. He was a grown man who lived with his grandmother and apparently had never lived on his own. He would stand in the employee's only doorway, yammering on to employees, who he is boring to tears, totally oblivious to the fact that this was our sanctuary. The back room was where we went to get away from all the crazies, but no, the crazies disregarded the employee's only sign and came on back to join us. They intruded upon us even when we were on a break, sometimes with a question but more likely just to socialize, once again totally unaware of how desperately we needed to get away from them.

I'm pretty sure Jameson had never had a girlfriend, or boyfriend for that matter. He had several times in the past been too friendly with the younger high-school or college girls on our staff. Several times he had stalked one or more of the girls on the staff, appearing at their windows at home at night or just appearing everywhere a particular girl happened to be. The stalking occurred before I began my employment here at the library, for surely I would have notified the police.

He did continue to make the young women on our staff uncomfortable and just flat out annoyed and grossed out the rest of us. He talked very loudly in this completely monotone, flat voice. He droned on as he talked about who lived in what house two hundred years ago. He wore really thick glasses, another frog peering through ice, but still couldn't see very well. He had a soft, fleshy, unmasculine physique. He was obsessed with war history.

He began showing up wearing a WW II Nazi Storm trooper uniform. I think we might have one Jewish family in this community. I wish we had others so that, maybe, enough people would be offended by him walking around town wearing it that something could be done. He should be ostracized for his insensitive choice in dress. I understand being into the war re-enactment, but to choose to wear a Nazi uniform around town has crazy written all over it.

Chapter Twenty-Six
Christian Fiction

Christian fiction should be reclassified as "reading light." This book genre gains more popularity daily. It is asked for more than any other type of fiction. Some of the reasons for that may be that a lot of the people who read this type of book either are not willing to look on their own for books or don't know how to find books in the library.

This particular fiction classification really bothers me. How exactly should Christian fiction look or how should it be plotted? Have you ever tried to read one of these books? To me, these books feed into the Thou-shalt-not-be-aware commandment, by which a growing segment of our population is choosing to live. The underpinnings of this quasi-Christian movement seem to be a need to have simple answers in a complicated, complex world. The themes of these books read like *The Waltons* and *Little House on the Prarie.* Laura Ingalls Wilder did write some beautiful books that many young girls still enjoy reading, but there comes a time when young girls and young boys become men and women and are supposed to want to become a part of the real, complicated, bewildering mess we call life. When a person moves away from what mom and dad taught and explores the worlds of art, literature, religion, culture, economics, etc., then he starts becoming his own person. Staying with *The Waltons* will not get one there.

I see so many adults who seem to suffer from arrested development. They still think Norman Rockwell is the best artist because they have never studied or immersed themselves in art. They stay with what is the most accessible. They think Danielle Steele and Christian Fiction are the best fiction because they refuse to open their minds to anything else. These are the same adults who consider meatloaf, and mashed potatoes and gravy the essence of good eating because they haven't tried anything else. Who would pass up good Greek, Italian, or Indian food for meatloaf except someone who hasn't tried the Greek, Italian, or Indian cuisine?

The Christian Fiction crowd will not read books with cuss words or sex scenes in them. They, for the most part, have not read the classics, such as Dickens, Faulkner, Hardy, Dreiser, Eliot, London. None of these would be familiar to them, nor would Dante or Milton or even C.S. Lewis.

Historical fiction offends them. I love reading about history.

These people are offended by the graphic language used by soldiers at war, which is a huge part of history. The descriptions of the unfortunates during the French Revolution would be merely offensive to them. It would not propel them to care more about others. No, they just don't want to be made aware of it. They want a sanitized version of pre-revolution Paris, even though, in reality, there isn't one. A Disney version of history is preferable to the real one. These are the same people who demanded an alternate version to the blockbuster film *Titanic*. They wanted a version with the sex scene omitted. How can a sex scene bother a person when, in that same movie, thousands of people who viewers have come to know and care about are going to die terrible deaths? Sex and nudity really bother these people, but gratuitous violence and tremendous suffering is okay. Don't get me wrong. A little modesty is good. A little inhibition helps keep the fabric of society together. But for adults to get so riled up over a sex scene seems childish and psychotic.

We have patrons asking us to pull magazines, books, and movies off the shelves on a regular basis because of alleged foul language, nudity, or sex scenes. We have pulled *Rolling Stone*, *Vanity Fair*, *Vogue*, and *Bride* because the covers have offended someone. I would have reminded the patron that these items are here for a variety of people to enjoy, and that this is not their personal library. We have pulled the *Sports Illustrated Swimsuit Edition* almost every year, since it offends someone. But the *Guns & Ammo* and *Hunting* magazines remain popular.

I have had a patron ask me to pull the newer, current installments of *Nancy Drew*. They want the *Nancy Drew* of 2007 to match the *Nancy Drews* of the 1950s. I agree that young adult culture has accelerated way too fast and that young adults are sexually maturing at too young an age. Their level of quasi-sophistication and materialism is overwhelming them and making it more likely that they will become involved in sexual activities, but I don't think *Nancy Drew* books are the problem. The marketing of sex in popular culture starts on television and trickles down into books, music, and fashion. Marketers have turned elementary-aged children into little name-brand consumers. Growing up in a college town, I didn't go to malls to hang out. They weren't meeting places for us. Materialism was deplored. Now a young adult's existence seems to center on who has the product with the most Nike swooshes on it.

So why aren't these parents who are so offended by nudity going after the real corrupters, the marketers and network executives who put inappropriate television shows on during children's hours and insert gratuitous violence on computer games and television shows? We know violence has a more negative effect on children than nudity.

I had a Christian patron tell me we needed to pull the movie depiction of E.M. Forster's *Room with a View*, a lovely handling of his marvelously subtle novel, because of a little nudity. My response was, "It is a lovely movie. Why are you focusing on the nudity?" I also reminded her that the film is in the adult section of the library, not the kids' section. The same request was made for the film version of Thomas Hardy's *Jude the Obscure.*

The Christian Fiction reminds me of elevator music. They take something great, literature and music, and water it down to make it more palatable to lesser brains. I see this happening in churches, too. The beautiful sacred music is now being synthesized into easy listening and light music. The words are sometimes even up on a screen in large letters with a little moving dot. I want my "Agnes Dei" to be sacred. I want my literature to be vibrant and full of complex characters and dialogue. I want my art to be done by inspired artists, not a Thomas Kinkaid wannabe. The genuine article becomes more elusive every day.

Chapter Twenty-Seven
Board Ethics

When I first became employed by the library there were two branches acting independently of each other. Both libraries served the entire county, but our library is the city library, and the other branch served the outlying townships and rural areas. Patrons could use either library. We shared our collections, but we did not share the same board. The county library was funded with county taxes, and the city library with city taxes. The county library was only an eighth the size of the city library. It has grown quite a bit within the last ten years because of a very generous patron donation, but it still only possesses about a quarter of the circulation the city library has.

The county library, even though it was, at this time, only an eighth the size of the city library with less than a quarter of the circulation, had a much more employee-friendly board governing it. Worker salaries were a third larger than ours over at the much bigger, busier city library.

When the possibility arose of the two libraries combining to become one entity, a lot of the city folks balked at this, since they knew the city people paid more taxes than the county folks, yet none of them knew or were made aware of the salary disparities. They may not have cared even if they had known. This is one area where this very fiscally conservative blue-collar towns exhibited a tremendous error of judgment. They seemed to think that since they lived on less than $10,000 a year as factory workers in the '50s, '60s and '70s, then so should everyone else in the twenty-first century. They also seemed to think that people were expendable, so if we workers weren't happy or satisfied they could easily be replaced.

I have yet to figure out why our society is so secretive when it comes to people's salaries. We all, for the most part, toil away at work for eight hours a day in exchange for money. Why aren't we candid about the very thing that keeps the world turning? It makes people so uncomfortable to talk about how much money they make. I think it would be healthy for us to make salaries public knowledge. Maybe the huge disparities between upper management and CEOs versus the rest of their employees would never have been allowed to become so tremendous if we had all been aware of what was happening. Maybe professional athletes wouldn't be making millions of dollars a year while teachers make $30,000 per year. The more aware we are of monetary inequality, the better.

So the vote to combine the two libraries was a hot topic. The board members from each library needed to be unanimous in order for this to happen. There was one city board member who put conditions on his vote. At this time there was a board member who was also an elementary school teacher who had not been able to secure a teaching position in our area, even though his wife was a teacher. He was local and well known. In this area, you almost have to be a local to get most jobs but especially a teaching position. This should have been a warning sign in itself. There was another board member who was a cranky, obtuse, contentious man who was on all kinds of boards and committees. You know the type. These people appear to me to be huge ego maniacs. Why do they feel a need to be on so many boards and committees? How do they have so much free time and feel their input is so important? In order for this cranky old board member to vote yes, his teacher buddy on the board had to become the children's librarian at the city library. I have to wonder if this was even legal. We all knew that ethically it was abominable. So the teacher board member resigned his position on the board and proceeded to become a lousy, uninspired, unmotivated children's librarian. After ten or fifteen years of doing absolutely nothing to enhance the children's program, while making twice the amount of money I was making at the time, along with full benefits, he came out of the closet, left his wife and two kids, and moved to a different state.

In my experience, when strings get pulled it's usually to the detriment of the company or organization that is taking on the employee pulled in by the string.

Have you ever noticed how some egos just need constant petting and managing? This board member's ego had to be placated constantly. He now has a room at the library named after him. Why did a cranky, mean person who could care less about the employees he supposedly governed get rewarded with recognition? It seems like it's always like this in our country. We give out this chintzy little reward/recognition to assuage the egos of the least deserving. Whatever happened to doing something good without reward or recognition?

This man finally left the library board, but he still brings his grouchy, ego-ridden self to the library several times a week, always looking like he's upset with everything. There will be five or six activities going on around him, but he'll still require a one-on-one talk with our director or assistant director. He is so self-absorbed that he cannot or will not see that we're all busy and cannot talk with him at that moment. It's as though he has to come in three times a week just to make sure the library is somehow surviving without him.

This type of attitude is prevalent in this small town. Maybe it is in all small towns, especially with the men. They have inflated senses of accomplishment that are not justified: the big fish in the small ponds. Never mind that half of them have never left this small town except maybe to go to college. There is one elderly male patron who's always going on and on about the house he built. One day he brought in a picture, and lo and behold, it's a glorified mobile home. He had simply added a shed-type building onto it. The old guys who sit and read the papers go on and on about their jobs at the John Deere or GM plants like they were on the verge of finding a cure for cancer. You don't hear the real movers and shakers of the world talking about them selves like this. It is pathetic to hear, and they will go on for hours. It's like masturbation of the mouth. And then they go on about their incredible pensions, totally unconcerned about the fact that my generation and their grandchildren probably will not have any pensions or social security at all.

They have told me their stories of how they laughed at Toyota and all the other Asian imports when they first came to America. It is this continued arrogance that has brought GM, Ford, and all the other American car manufacturers to their knees.

Who's laughing now?

Chapter Twenty-Eight
Paper Thief

The library had copies of a variety of newspapers for everyone to read on the premises. They were not to be taken from the library. We normally didn't put targets on papers. We relied on patrons to simply not take them based on the honor system.

At one point, the "Travel and Leisure" section was regularly missing. We all kept an eye out on the paper readers but were never able to find out who the thief was. Now remember, this was the "Travel and Leisure" section of the paper.

So it was decided that a target would be placed in the paper. Well, one day the alarm went off and the paper thief was discovered, a retired man who had a very generous pension package. In other words, he had plenty of money. A person stealing the "Travel and Leisure" section may end up in Dante's worst section of Hell. On the other hand, anyone would understand someone needing to steal the "Help Wanted" section of the paper.

Our assistant director went to talk with the thief as he was stupidly standing in the alarm. He had the paper folded up in his pocket. She asked him if he had something in his pocket. He proceeded to take it out and pretended he didn't know he couldn't take part of the paper.

We had had a variety of other paper thieves who would steal certain sections. Our directors decided to go ahead and reward these thieves by allowing them to have free copies of the section of the paper they were stealing.

Chapter Twenty-Nine
Hunters as Conservationists

We have men and women come into the library in full camouflage (including a painted camouflage face) looking for maps that will show them where public lands are and where they can hunt. They'll come into the library with blood on them from previous hunts. They'll have deer roped to their cars or trucks. It's disgusting.

Michigan hunters are allowed to hunt on public land. This means they are allowed to hunt in state parks where families go walking together on weekends. I've heard gunshots as I walked through the beautiful woods with my kids and dogs beside me. It's as though I have entered the twilight zone. I don't know what other states allow, but it shouldn't be allowed anywhere. If you intend to hunt, then buy lots of land. If you can't afford it, don't hunt. There are plenty of activities I would like to participate in, but I can't afford to do and therefore don't get to do. These hunters are allowed to shoot guns in the same areas where people are walking. Does this not seem like one of the most ridiculous situations ever?

Hasn't hunting outlived its purpose? We really don't need to hunt for food anymore. Our civilization has moved beyond that.

I had never met anyone who hunted until I moved to Michigan. The first day I went downtown there were dead deer hanging up on a pole right downtown. I immediately went up to the high school where my husband teaches and told him I was moving back to North Carolina. I know North Carolina has hunters, but the area of North Carolina I had lived in didn't. I didn't want to live among people who considered killing of any kind a sport. Still don't want to. I'd like to see all the avid hunter-people who like to kill sent over to fight our wars. Killing for sport is not something human beings should want to do.

How can a grown person be proud of him or herself for killing defenseless animals and then stuffing them and putting them on a wall? There are people here who have stuffed animals all over their houses, even stuffed turkeys! There are so many hunters that the high schools close on the opening day of hunting season! It is not safe to walk in the woods for at least six weeks in autumn, the most beautiful time to be in the woods. And no one does anything about it, since a majority of the population hunts.

When I think of conservation, I think of conserving a forest and the inhabitants for their own sakes. That's how I have always thought of conservation. But here, the forest and forest dwellers, along with aquatic life, are conserved and controlled because of what they can provide. Lakes, ponds, wildlife, forests, rivers aren't appreciated simply for their majesty and beauty, or because we need them simply to survive; they are "maintained" by conservationists so there will be hunting and fishing aplenty. This goes totally against the principles of what I had considered conservation. This view of conservation is totally selfish. There is no value placed on the forest's wildlife. They just want to make sure there are enough critters out there for them to have something to shoot at and kill.

Most hunters pull the trigger when something moves. It could be a child or a dog. They'll kill any dog if it's chasing a deer, since it made killing the deer impossible for them. What causes a human being to become trigger happy? And what are they doing living with the rest of us?

If they can't find public land some of them will go ahead and hunt on private land. They'll just pull off the side of the road, grab their guns and go. It's like living in the Wild West.

Chapter Thirty
Short People, Stiff People

All of you tall, agile people are going to go crazy over this. Apparently the short, out of shape, patrons complained so much about not being able to reach the books on the top shelves or bend over to reach the books on the bottom shelves that it was decided we would no longer use the top and bottom shelves.

Patrons can ask any one of us to get a book for them. I would much rather they ask for help than limit the number of books we have by eliminating shelves. This really does not seem remotely fair to the rest of the population. Plus, if you can't bend your knees or bend over, you really need to at least try.

Doesn't this reinforce the idea that we are accommodating the weaker, less intelligent, less healthy, and in doing so we are taking away from the people who excel and take care of themselves? I realize that eventually everyone ends up with stiff bones from aging. When this happens to me, I would rather ask an employee to help me rather than have the entire bottom shelf of books removed so that I don't have to encounter an obstacle.

Chapter Thirty-One
Strange Requests, Odd Situations

One day an elderly hillbilly and his hillbilly son came walking up to the front desk. They asked for a document from the 1800s. He really thought I would be able to produce a document from two centuries ago.

Another strange request: around Christmas last year a patron wanted to get one of the bums from the wall of bums a pair of pants. She wanted me to find out what size pants he wore.

Almost every book on résumé writing and how to go about finding a job or taking the GED is never returned; in other words they're stolen by just the kind of person you'd want to hire.

We cannot keep witchcraft, Wicca, or abortion books in the library. We don't know if the witches are taking the books or if the turbo-Christians are taking the books. They just disappear.

Frequently, the old, grizzly, haven't-taken-a-bath-in-a-month men in overalls come in to use our bathrooms and don't bother to close the door. No inhibitions at all.

We regularly have children who come into the library straight from school and stay until we close at eight o'clock.

With their children, we have parents show up after school drunk or with alcohol on their breath.

We have had a criminal, who had just murdered his grandmother six hours before, come into the library to use our computers, and as he was leaving, steal our donation jar with cash in it. One of our staff, not knowing this person was a murderer, ran after him shouting, "Stop, that money is for the children!" He was arrested several hours later. That's when we found out he was a murderer.

We run the public access channel from the library. We have several patrons who have their religious programs broadcast on public access. Since we broadcast it, it is always on, but usually with the volume all the way down so we can maintain our sanity. There is one middle-aged woman who has her very own Bible study featured on public access. If only you all could hear her. It makes one wonder what kind of life she must have led to become so screwed up. The icing on the cake though, is her vanity license plate which reads MY LORD'S. She drives a big-ass Cadillac to make the icing sweeter. No doubt the Lord would want her to be gobbling up extra natural resources with her Cadillac. Have you noticed how the turbo-Christians are now attributing their financial success to the Lord? As if the Lord has blessed some with wealth but not others. I seriously doubt the Lord picks and chooses who's going to be rich and who's going to be poor. I do know that the Lord would be furious if he ever came to visit us and saw the conditions lived in by the poor. I am pretty sure He would be very angry with all the rich folk who had justified their greediness by convincing themselves that the Lord had blessed them by enabling them to become wealthy.

We have several families who are Pentecostal Christians. They do not allow their girls to wear pants or cut their hair or wear bathing suits. These daughters cannot play sports in school, since they can't wear pants. Personally, I think this constitutes child abuse.

One of the Pentecostal fathers happens to be a Biology professor at our small community college. First of all, I have to wonder why a Fundamentalist Christian would have any interest in biology, much less pursue biology as a career. This professor refuses to teach Darwinism in his biology classes. Yes, you read this correctly. Darwin is to Biology what Bach is to Music. Are you wondering at this very moment how this can possibly be allowed? I am too. Why wouldn't the thousands of parents who have had kids take that class object? This college gets state money, too.

Denialville is a very conservative Republican community only when it is convenient. One of the most outstanding features of Republicanism is a small, non-interfering government, and yet when it comes to bail-outs, helping-hands, and corporate welfare, they accept it all. The businesses here are always requesting tax abatements. They feel that since they provide jobs, they should get more breaks. Well, the only way to run most businesses is by hiring employees. That is part of the arrangement. So why do they feel they are doing something that needs to be rewarded?

The State of Michigan is offering grants for our downtown business owners to help with the beautification and restoration of our downtown businesses. Why should the state pay for this and why would a Republic business owner feel that accepting government money for something he should be responsible for is ethical?

Our local paper at some point featured an editorial about the possibility of our government lying. There were at least four responses from readers who remarked that certainly our government never has or ever would lie to us. These were individuals who are old enough to have lived through The Vietnam War, Watergate and of course our current administration. One again, *Thou shalt not be aware.* This unwillingness or inability to become aware is crippling our country.

Our childhood leukemia and cancer rates are very high. My son's class of 200 has 8 cases of childhood leukemia. No one looked into why; they simply held bake sales to help with medical expenses. I called the manager at our local paper and asked if he would put an investigative journalist on this horrible situation. He asked me if I knew in fact it was high, and I told him it didn't take

Sherlock Holmes to figure out that it was. He told me I could look into that on my own if I was interested in it. Once again, denial and an unwillingness to know the truth, since there might be jobs lost at the chemical factory. A handful of kids getting cancer seems worth the trade off to the people on this town.

We do not get movies that challenge the mind here in Denialville. We normally get Disney, Claude Van Dam type action movies, or not very witty or smart comedies. Those of you living in areas who get great films have no idea what it is like not to get these fabulous films. This does not reflect the preferences of the managers of the theaters; it reflects the tastes and sensibilities of the population here. They do not want to watch anything that involves thinking or awareness. Because of this, I wanted to have a film festival here at the library so at least the population here would have a chance to see good, thought-provoking films. Whether or not a person shares the same opinions shouldn't be the criteria used when deciding to see a movie. Denialville has not had any of the Michael Moore films brought to its theaters. This in itself is outrageous, but the fact that Mr. Moore is from Flint, Michigan, which is only several hours away from Denialville, makes it sickening. He is practically a native son, and yet his movies are not made available and no one seems to care. So I wanted to present his films, along with the Zeitgeist Films production of Mark Achbar and JenniferAbbott's *The Corporation* along with *Who Killed the Electric Car* along with others. This would at least give people in this town a chance to see these films without having to drive several hours to an out-of-town theater. My director axed the idea but told me I could show old movies instead. I think a library's primary responsibility is to enlighten, edify, and educate, especially in areas like this where enlightenment is hard to find.

Chapter Thirty-Two
Becca's Transformation

This chapter is written by one of the high school pages who work at the library. She is a delightful, positive, effervescent young woman. After working one summer full time, her entire attitude towards humanity changed, as you will read for yourself.

"Will you help me find a book?" Before an answer can be given, a refusal on the basis of work and other inconsequential things, the child slips his hand into hers and leads her up the ramp into the children's section of the library. He speaks quickly and animatedly as he releases her hand in favor of darting about the aisles to find the most attractive-looking book. Seizing upon one he trots back to her, eyes alight at the prospect of being read to. She smiles and sits, acquiescing to his question, asked with glowing smile and slightly squinted eyes. The boy pulls out his own chair after handing the teen the book, squirming to get closer to the opening pages and flowering colors.

She reads, voice keeping time with the words as she takes them in and lets them out. They flow smoothly, river water rushes and gurgles along with the illustrations, and the child is enamored with the night-time ritual she enjoyed as a child. He scoots closer and laughs when he finds something funny, pouts when the tale doesn't follow the path he has set for it mentally. Just before the story's close, another child wanders over.

"I'm getting all *these* books," proudly placing the stack on the corner of the square table before sitting down, eyes already fixed on the open book the teen has set down.

"You can do that?" the boy exclaims, somewhat indignantly, disbelief evident.

"You just have to have a library card, and you can check out as many books as you like," the teenager tells him, smiling.

"My mom won't get me one: she's evil." He said it so matter of factly that the tale teller laughs as the latecomer cocks her head to the side, not understanding a mother not allowing her child to borrow books. The teen finishes the book, and pardons herself.

"Those books aren't going to shelve themselves, you know. If it gets slow I'll come back up and read some more." She never does make it back up, but she does keep an eye on the boy, whom she guesses to be no more than ten, as he stays for two and a half hours. She pops up; standing on toes' tips and cranes her neck to spot him as he explores the library, doing her job as a library page.

The job not mentioned on the contract: being the babysitter of children, kids six to thirteen, who are dropped off at the library so parents can be rid of them for a few hours with free babysitting.

The library is not the place of book lovers. It is the shelter of bums, a place of water fountains, public bathrooms, soft chairs, free computer time, and shelter from the elements. The library is just another name for daycare, a place where your frustrations can easily be taken out against the minimum-wage teenagers that man the desk, the hub for the dregs of humanity, a place where you can hit and yank about your child as if you were home, a place to show off your mail-order brides to the horrified and indignant staff. Hell, a place to mentally abuse and degrade your fiancé.

They come for the computers, for the bathrooms, for the occasional book that they will lose and have to piteously wheedle their way out of paying for. They lie to get more free prints, refuse to pay, and leave when they are told they owe twenty cents for copies, and think nothing of it. The mentally handicapped come in and stay for hours at a time, the mothers that should not have children parade in with their six children that run amok as they, the parents, attach themselves to the computer.

Hush! This is a library.

It is rarely quiet or relaxing.

Epilogue

I hope after reading this book you are convinced of the far-reaching consequences we all face when we allow active addicts and alcoholics, individuals with psychotic mental illnesses, and people with low IQs to have children.

I know, to a lot of you, this sounds like eugenics. I have to wonder if those of you against eugenics are aware of the human suffering brought about by poor parenting.

We have an adoption book at the library. It has pictures of children waiting to be adopted. They range in age from two to seventeen. Can you imagine what it does to a child to never, ever, during its entire life have had anyone who wants it? Can you seriously not believe this child would have been better off not being born? There are thousands of these kids smiling at the camera so someone will want them, love them, and take care of them.

We all know that if there isn't someone there to bond with a child during the first six weeks of life, the child will suffer irreparable emotional damage. Even couples who have adopted infants recognize there could be, and probably will be, emotional or behavioral problems.

Are those of you against eugenics willing to adopt an unwanted child? There are thousands of them out there. These would be children who are scarred emotionally. No matter how much love, time, attention, consistency, and discipline you give them, they will never be able to overcome the abuse, neglect, or abandonment experienced at the beginning of their lives. Are you prepared to adopt a child born with fetal alcohol syndrome, whose low IQ will inhibit him from leading any kind of normal, happy life? What are your suggested solutions to all this human misery? All the love, money, and compassion in the world will never cure it.

The children in the state adoption book have been in and out of foster homes most of their lives and living in hell before getting there, since we all know parents practically have to kill children before they are taken away. They will be wards of the state until they are eighteen years old and beyond. Most of them will end up in jail, where we will continue to pour more resources into a life that has never been given what it takes to be human. We spend more money on prisons than we do on education.

It would be great to see all the people against eugenics and abortion devote their time, talents, and energy on getting some type of legislation passed that would bring about a more serious attitude toward parenthood. Why do we allow it to be so easy to become a parent when it involves something as precious as a life? We could eliminate so much human suffering simply by becoming more aware of the consequences of allowing anyone and everyone to have children.

What is wrong with requiring a person to be at least twenty-one before having a child? What is wrong with a person needing to have at least an average IQ before having a child? What is wrong with requiring potential parents to prove they can support themselves and a child? And what about blood tests to make sure a person doesn't have AIDS to pass on to their child, or doesn't practice active drug and alcohol use, which we know causes FAS? We need to require psychiatric evaluations to ensure a parent does not have any type of mental illness that would cause him or her to neglect or endanger a child. What is wrong with making sure people are sane and competent before they have children?

The Foster Parent Review Board holds its meetings here at the library. Any person planning to become a foster parent meets with the Review Board to be considered and evaluated. You should see the people who show up to be considered. Believe me, you wouldn't want to leave your pets with most of these people. I'm sure there are some people who make great foster parents, and our thanks go out to them, but the majority of foster-parents simply see it as a government handout and could care less about the children. The Board can't afford to be too picky because "pickin's are slim" out there, so the requirements for becoming a foster-parent are minimal.

Handing out money to welfare families when they choose to have more kids is not the answer. Shouldn't adults be responsible for their own actions? Needing welfare to help with one child while a person is getting a life back together is understandable. That's what welfare is there for, not to become a way of life. Allowing herself to become pregnant while on welfare should not entitle a woman to more money. That behavior entitles her to a big dunce cap. I think a large segment of our population feels this way, but we have just given up voicing our opinions.

We need to force our government to focus on why there are so many children born with mental and physical handicaps. Most educated people realize our environment plays a big role in producing children with emotional and behavioral problems. Our food, water, and air are practically unfit for human consumption. Businesses are not going to clean up their acts voluntarily. Our government has to force them to do it now, not ten years from now. We need to have a government that is not pro-business. We need a government that will tell the truth and do the right thing, no matter what the cost is to the economy. What good is a healthy economy if the air you breathe, the food you eat, and the water you drink causes cancer and mental retardation?

We also need to require countries to practice birth control before they receive aid. Why do we send African women just enough food so that they can menstruate and become pregnant again? They need birth control for themselves. They can't rely on the men to wear condoms. These women may be able to feed one baby, but instead they end up having litters of children. I am tired of seeing African children with bloated stomachs and flies swarming all over them. Why doesn't someone suggest that they simply not have children? If what we as a country have been doing for the past fifty years isn't working, maybe it's time to try a new approach. World population needs to be everyone's concern, but instead, no one seems the least bit concerned.

Ask yourself, should it be easier to have a child than it is to obtain a driver's license?

Those of you living in areas where other people's stupidity seems like it doesn't affect you, it does. The fallout affects us all. Do any of us want a child to suffer because of its parents? Do any of us want to continue throwing our money down the drain of a non-working welfare system that only allows adults to avoid taking responsibility for their actions?

I was in line behind a food-stamp customer at the grocery store the other day. Nowadays, if a person is using food stamps, he has a card that resembles a credit card instead of the good-ole book of stamps that everyone can see and hear as the purchaser rips them out to use them. I guess this is an attempt to eliminate the stigma or humiliation attached to food-stamp recipients.

Once again I'll say, humiliation is a good motivator for change. For some reason, on this particular day at the grocery store, the transaction with the food stamp card would not go through. The cashier started saying such things as, "That's your state government for you," and generally excoriating the state and federal governments, as if it is the governments' responsibility to feed families. This was especially bizarre, since the state of Michigan is practically bankrupt and our federal government is borrowing money every day from China for an outrageous war. These people had come to expect their state to feed them and had become angry when their food stamp card didn't work.

We need to rethink what compassionate behavior is. What is more compassionate, to allow someone to have a child who can't take care of it and to continue to support the person so she can have more children or to simply not let the pregnancy happen in the beginning? No matter how much money we pour into these children's crazy homes, there isn't any hope for them. No matter how much money we pour into public schools, it will not help these kids learn what they need to learn. A person cannot learn when depressed, and a human cannot come from a dysfunctional home without depression or some other learning, emotional, or behavioral problem. As my Hungarian grandfather used to say, "You can't make chicken salad out of chicken shit."

To illustrate how profound and widespread the effects are of letting incompetent humans have children, look at these few statistics from my son's elementary school. There are about three hundred kids at this school. Ninety percent of kids qualify for free lunch. Eighty-five percent live with someone other than their biological parents, usually the grandparents. Now remember, these grandparents are the parents who raised the crazy parents. The circle is complete with crazy people.

From what I am told, these statistics are similar to most elementary schools around the country, with the exception of those in affluent areas. When I read this I was astounded, disgusted, and depressed. Unless we do something about this, it will continue to go on and be considered acceptable.

So just remember, while you are working forty hours or more to make ends meet, it's likely that two crazy people whose combined IQs might be 100, with no jobs or job possibilities, are copulating without birth control, because it's free and easy.

About the Author

Ann Miketa grew up in Chapel Hill, North Carolina. She has lived in at least eight different states including Colorado, California, and Idaho, where she lived in a bus called "the House of Good Trips" with a group of alternative thinkers attempting to live communally. But in all her travels, nowhere has she encountered crazier people than those her sister introduced her to in the Library Diaries. She went to the University of North Carolina, Chapel Hill. She is currently working on her memoir.

Printed in the United States
124878LV00002B/124-210/P